BURY THE PAST, BUT SHOOT IT FIRST

BURY THE PAST, BUT SHOOT IT FIRST

I FEAR NO EVIL BOOK TWO

MARTHA CARR

MICHAEL ANDERLE

DISRUPTIVE IMAGINATION

BURY THE PAST, BUT SHOOT IT
FIRST TEAM

Thanks to the JIT Readers

John Ashmore
Jim Caplan
Peter Manis
Kelly O'Donnell
Paul Westman
Micky Cocker

If we've missed anyone, please let us know!

DEDICATIONS

From Martha

To everyone who still believes in magic
and all the possibilities that holds.
To all the readers who make this
entire ride so much fun.
And to my son, Louie and the wonderful Katie
who remind me all the time of what
really matters and how wonderful
life can be in any given moment.

From Michael

To Family, Friends and
Those Who Love
To Read.
May We All Enjoy Grace
To Live The Life We Are
Called.

I *do not have time for this shit.* The thought rolled through Shay's mind as she stepped out of Olio Pizzeria. She wanted a little quality pizza before she headed to her meeting at the Leanan Sídhe, the Irish pub where she would meet James Brownstone, the *bodyguard* the Professor was forcing on her for her upcoming job.

Instead, she had to deal with six assholes with skull tattoos chilling in the parking lot, waiting for her, grinning as she stepped out of the place. A nervous old man hurried by them, but they ignored him.

They were all members of a local gang, the Demon Generals. She'd tried to make a reasonable point with them about not shaking down her local pizzeria. Her restraint had backfired, it seemed.

Should have just killed them the first time. Then again, murdering three people and expecting some random pizza shop guy to clean it up might be too much. Not everyone's been killing since they were 15.

Shay let out an annoyed groan and rubbed the back of

her neck. She just wanted a normal life. Well, as normal a life as anyone could manage when they hunted down magical artifacts for a living, but when she was not on the job, she wanted to be able to go out for pizza without having to worry about if she was going to have to kill anyone.

Is this the universe's way of telling me, "Once a killer, always a killer?" Whatever.

One of the gang members took a few steps toward her but kept his distance. Smarter than they looked.

"Hey, *bitch*. You must be the one my homies told me about."

"I have no idea what you're talking about." Shay wasn't afraid of any of these assholes. She could kill them with ease, but she also didn't want to have a fight in an open parking lot.

"Nah, it's got to be you. No other hot-ass tail that hits the place up except you, bitch."

Shay glanced back at the squeak of the front door behind her opening. The pale-faced owner wiped some sweat off of his forehead.

"Should I call the police?"

The gang member in charge frowned. "You think the police can get here before we cap your ass, man?"

The owner's face twitched.

Shay let out a long sigh. She'd never intended to get involved in this sort of problem. All she cared about was making sure one of her favorite local pizza places didn't go under. It'd be nice if the Demon Generals could go harass some doughnut shops instead.

Why do I have a feeling I'm eventually gonna have to kill every single person in that gang?

"Don't worry about it." Shay pointed toward a nearby alley. "I think me and these gentlemen are gonna have a little discussion. No reason to get the police involved in a nice friendly chat between men and a woman sharing a mutual respect for one another."

The Demon Generals all laughed.

"Yeah, that's it." The lead Demon strutted back and forth. "Just a fucking little chat over tea and crumpets, bitch." He grabbed his crotch.

Shay kept her gaze locked on the gang members but kept speaking to the owner. "I suggest not coming out and checking on that alley for a while, no matter what you hear. If the police ask you anything later, just say you don't know shit. It'll be better for you and everyone else involved."

"Yeah," the gang member said. "Bitch has a point. You don't know shit."

The owner nodded and hurried back inside.

The gang members all chuckled, already sure of the ending.

Their representative nodded toward the alley. "Let's go, bitch. If you make us all happy over there, we can forget about what you did to our boys."

Shay rolled her eyes and considered how an oversupply of testosterone could reduce a man to a complete fucking idiot. Without saying another word, she headed toward the alley. The Demon Generals fell in behind her a few yards out.

She waited until they were safely ensconced in the alley

to reach into her jacket pocket and activated a short-range drone jammer. Her survey of the area revealed no cameras within line of sight.

"So, here's how this is gonna go," Shay said. "I'm gonna kill all of you. I thought about leaving you alive, but once your gang hears you're all dead, they'll *understand* not to fuck with me again."

"You stupid bitch. You think you can kill us all? We've gonna fuck you up and then we're going to take our time fucking you. Got me? Then you'll know why no one messes with the Demon Generals."

The gang members all laughed. Several started pounding their fists into their palms and licking their lips. Shay assumed they were trying for intimidating, but the whole thing came off rather desperate.

She offered them a thin smile "Not gonna walk away? Last chance. Makes no difference to me, assholes, if you live or die."

"You fucking bitch, I'm tired of this." The gang's leader rushed at her, cocking back his fist. "I'm gonna enjoy hearing your scream..."

His eyes widened, and only a soft gagging made it past the knife Shay jammed in his throat.

Shay didn't wait for the other men to recover from their shock. She pulled the blade out and pushed the man toward two of the others before charging a third.

The poor asshole went for his gun, but Shay slammed her knife into his heart right as his fingers grasped it. She held him as a shield and yanked the man's gun up. Three quick shots sent his friends to the ground.

The last man left alive managed to squeeze off two

rounds, but Shay's dying gang member meat shield took the bullets for her.

You need guns with better penetration, assholes.

She shot the gun out of the other man's hand, let the body she'd been holding fall, and advanced on the remaining gang member.

"You know what the best part about all of this is?" Shay grinned, getting close to the last man standing.

The wide-eyed gangster shook his head.

"When the police investigate, they aren't gonna dig at all. They're just gonna think some other pieces of street trash took you out."

"Look, you don't have to kill me, you know? I'll go back to my boys and tell them to leave you alone. I can make sure you never have any trouble with the Demon Generals ever again, you know?"

Shay narrowed her eyes. "I already tried being nice, and all it got me was six assholes looking to kill me. So now I'm gonna go back to a proven solution." She put a round into the man's head.

"Fucking idiots," she muttered as she fished a handkerchief out of her pocket to wipe her prints off the gun. She tossed it into the pile of slain gang members and searched for any witnesses. No one was around, but she assumed the cops would come soon enough to investigate the sound of the gunshots.

Time to go. I have a fucking meeting anyway.

"When is your guy gonna get here, Smite-Williams?" Shay said. She looked at the entrance to the Irish pub for the fifth time in the last couple of minutes.

The already drunk old man smiled and took a gulp of his beer. "Soon, Miss Carson. He's not late. You're just *early.*"

Shay bit down a snarky response and drummed her fingers against the table, her neck and shoulders tight. If her meeting hadn't been preceded by a massacre, she would have been less tense.

Kill six assholes, and I don't even get paid for it. Great.

Even without that, she would have been annoyed. Part of gaining control of her life meant also managing all the variables influencing it. She was technically supposed to be dead, and the more people she worked with, the greater the chance that deception might be revealed to the parties who had wanted her six feet in the ground.

Her research assistant Peyton, questionable fashion sense aside, was a competent man who had every reason to keep her secret given she'd helped him escape his own hit.

This Brownstone, though, everything Peyton dug up suggested the man was a kickass bounty hunter, and *religious* as well. A man like that wouldn't want to work with her, not if he knew the kind of woman she was before being a tomb raider.

Shay wasn't about to reveal her true background to the bounty hunter, but if she could get him off the job, that'd reduce her risk.

She cleared her throat. "I'm still telling you I don't need this Brownstone. Not really. It's just an extra body and extra trouble."

The Professor chuckled. "The Red Warlocks might disagree. They aren't to be taken lightly, Miss Carson."

"Neither am I. They wouldn't be the first people flinging around magic that I've taken down during a tomb raid."

"Oh, I don't doubt that at all, but you have to see this from my perspective. I need the artifact."

"I'll get you the artifact. I'm just saying I don't need a babysitter."

"And as I've explained before. This is non-negotiable." The Professor gave her a cheerful smile. "Don't worry, Miss Carson. Your compensation is completely independent of James."

Shay spotted Brownstone the instant he entered the bar. She'd already seen pictures of him online, but as he made his way toward the booth, she took the moment to look him over carefully.

Odd birthmarks and ridges covered his rugged face. She wouldn't say it made him ugly, but he was about as far from classically handsome as you could get. Hints of tattoos peeked out from underneath his sleeves and collar. His thick muscles strained against his shirt and pants.

Woah. This guy is cut. He's like a statue come to life.

Brownstone carried an old moleskin notebook. Something about it struck Shay as incongruent with the rest of musclebound image the bounty hunter had going.

Smite-Williams gestured to an empty seat across from him and Brownstone sat down. He took a good, long look at Shay.

The woman never had any problems appreciating that she was hot as the surface of the sun. It'd been a useful tool during her time as a killer, and it was the rare man who didn't appreciate her lush dark hair, beautiful face, and athletic body.

Time to poke him a little and see what kind of man he is. Reputation is just a bunch of rumors in the end.

Shay smirked. "Like what you see, big man?"

"Just wondering who you are."

Disappointment stabbed Shay. The least the bastard could do was show a little mutual appreciation for her appearance. She liked what she saw, after all, and it's not like she didn't know she was hot.

"Sure, pal." Shay rolled her eyes. "Keep telling yourself that."

The last thing she would do was let this Brownstone end up thinking he had control of the conversation.

The bounty hunter ignored her. Instead, he opened his notebook and pulled out a pen.

What the fuck? Whatever. I'll figure out his deal later.

The Professor cleared his throat. "James Brownstone, this is Shay Carson. I'll tell you her role in this once I explain the job."

Brownstone nodded, his gaze flicking to her for an instant but not lingering.

"And before I can go into the job," the Professor said, "I need to give you a little history lesson."

"My least-favorite subject," Brownstone muttered.

Shay snorted. "Why am I not surprised?"

Brownstone is just a meathead in the end, all muscle and no brain, my least favorite kind of man, let alone partner for a job.

Peyton might be worthless when it came to field work and kicking ass, but at least the man had a dangerous brain.

The Professor glanced between them and shook his head. "Play nice, you two. You each provide complimentary skills for this job." He waved a hand. "Anyway, James, are you familiar with the Cartagena Codex?"

The bounty hunter shook his head. "Nope."

Shay resisted a laugh. She must have been smirking because Smite-Williams shot her an angry glare. She shrugged but didn't respond.

I can't help it if your boy is all muscle and no brain.

"It's a rather recent discovery. From what has been decoded, it was apparently written after the conquest of the Inca Empire by Pizzaro, by what may have been refugees who had resettled in a small surviving Mayan city." The Professor took a sip of his beer.

I better interpret for Brownstone. He probably has no clue of some of the importance of what he's being told.

"The Incas didn't have a full writing system, you see. The Mayans did."

Brownstone shrugged like he already knew that. Shay doubted it.

The Professor leaned forward, folding his hands in front of him. "The point is, lad, that unlike most other codices from the early periods, this one wasn't destroyed. It was transported from its city of origin and eventually ended up hidden in what is now Cartagena, Colombia. And it tells an interesting story."

"A *very* interesting story," Shay added. She shifted in her seat. The bounty hunter didn't care about history, but she did, and she could already kick ass.

I'm being too hard on the guy, but I'm gonna prove to him

that I don't need someone like him for a tomb raid. I've got all the team I need already with Peyton.

Brownstone glanced over at Shay, a slightly confused look on his face.

"A lot of what's in that codex might not have been believed twenty years ago," said Smite-Williams. "From what can be deciphered, it tells a story of Pizzaro gaining control of an ancient artifact, a rod that was supposed to be associated with the Inca god Supay, God of Death and the Underworld. His name is also associated with a race of demons, and the codex implies that Pizzaro actually made use of the artifact to summon dark creatures to aid him in fighting Inca forces."

"Bet they left that out of the reports back to Spain," Brownstone muttered.

Okay, that was funny. Captain Muscles has a little more going on upstairs than I thought. Time for the real test, though.

"You'll love what they were called," Shay added with a wink.

Brownstone shrugged. "All right, what were they called?"

"The closest translation would be 'corpse-demons that walk again.'"

"Goddamn motherfucking zombies," Brownstone spat. "Why does it have to be zombies?"

"Motherfucking zombies," Shay echoed.

She was doing the job for the sweet pile of cash Smite-Williams was going to throw at her, but she could admit to herself that she liked the idea of keeping a zombie rod out of general circulation.

"Aye, lad, zombies." The Professor grinned. "Now, when

you have your ear to the ground like I do, you hear a lot of things, and you can begin to piece disparate things together. Long story short, I have good information on the location of the Rod of Supay."

Does Brownstone understand how impressive it is that the Professor can zero in on the location of a long-lost artifact like that. Probably not. The thought disappointed her more than she expected.

Brownstone took a deep breath and nodded. He looked a little uncomfortable. *Zombies freak him out.*

The Professor nodded toward Shay. "This is where Miss Carson comes in. She's a field archaeologist with good tactical skills. Considering the nature of this particular mission, that's a good combination."

"She's a graverobber who can use a gun," Brownstone joked.

The graverobber quip stung a bit, but she wasn't going to whine about it. The best way to fight jokes was with other jokes.

"That or a kickass treasure hunter. I think the politically correct term is *tomb raider*." Shay smirked. "It's not always graves, you know. But I'm okay around weapons. Not like we live in a safe world, especially these days."

"This time your skills will be particularly helpful, Miss Shay, and convenient." The Professor turned toward Brownstone. "We have a strong lead on the Rod that suggests it's buried in a tomb complex in northern Peru. It's been explored before, but we have reasons—many reasons, actually—to believe the Rod was magically shielded from detection, and there are no active excavations going on due to issues at the site and local rebel activity. Shay will be taking lead on this, and you'll be support."

"Unless you have a problem following a woman?" There was defiance in Shay's eyes.

This would be the main test. The Professor might have not left her much choice in Brownstone tagging along, but she wanted to make it clear that this was *her* job, and he was the tagalong.

"Fine by me." Brownstone jotted down a few more notes and looked back up at Shay.

She tried to hide the residual irritation. She didn't like working with anyone in the field, but he didn't take any chance she offered to try and annoy her. She had to give him a little credit.

So, he's not easy to spin up. That's good to know. It means he won't be a bitch when we're traveling together.

Brownstone turned his attention to the Professor. "That I'm being invited to the party implies this isn't just about digging up some moldy zombie rod. There's a bounty involved."

"Well, yes, James. Some others are interested in the Rod of Supay," Smite-Williams said, his smile faltering for a moment.

"Who?"

"The *Brujos Rojos*."

Brownstone leaned back and nodded, his face twitching slightly. "I thought they got taken out when they tried to assassinate that high-ranking Light Elf during her visit to Colombia last year."

Shay didn't hate magic, but she couldn't ignore that it's reentry into the world had led to assholes who would have been nothing before now being dangerous threats. Then again, magic also made her job very, very profitable.

Even if she didn't like it, she could see the advantage that having an extra gun around might provide. Her recent fight with Snegurka the Ice Witch wasn't the one-sided curb stomp Shay would have preferred. That didn't mean she couldn't take the Warlocks by herself but having Brownstone to take their attention off her would make it easy for her to kill them.

"Not enough of them were finished off," the Professor explained. "They've been recruiting, and now they're sniffing around the Rod of Supay. Whatever our various motivations for being interested in this artifact are, none of us wants a group of homicidal Warlocks to get their hands on it."

Brownstone gave the Professor a curt nod. "I'm in." He frowned as something occurred to him. "On one condition."

Shay peered at the bounty hunter, wondering if he was more worried about the Warlocks than he appeared.

"What is that?" the Professor asked, a curious glint in his eye. "Don't get greedy now, lad. You get to make money and kick some evil ass. Isn't that enough?"

Brownstone snorted. "My dog is missing. I'd like you to look for him while I'm on the job."

Shay had to resist bursting out in laughter. Mister Class Six Super Bounty Hunter was worried about Fido when they had to go recover a zombie rod.

The mirth faded, and she found herself confused, an uncomfortable feeling. She realized something very important. She didn't understand Brownstone. Not at all.

Being a killer was as much about human psychology as it was combat skills. A professional needed to think about a mark and how they might react in a situation.

Shay prided herself on her ability to understand and evaluate people, even if she accepted that most people weren't that complicated. Brownstone, though, hadn't reacted at all like she'd expected. It was like he'd lodged a splinter in her mind.

The Professor chuckled. "And here I thought you were going to ask for something much more expensive." He nodded at Shay. "Well, Miss Carson, it looks like you have support." He clapped his hands together. "And now, I do believe this is the part of the evening where Father O'Banion comes out to play."

Shay stretched. Brownstone glanced over at her for a second before scribbling down a few notes.

Shay scowled at him, annoyed that the man left her so confused. He shrugged at her.

I'll have plenty of time to figure you out on this trip, Brownstone.

2

The Professor flagged down a waitress to ask for three Guinness draughts.

"Are all those for you?" Brownstone glanced up at the Professor.

Shay managed not to snort but was glad Brownstone asked. The Professor knew his shit when it came to artifacts, but Shay was closing on the opinion that he lived his life as a functional alcoholic. Either that, or when it was time to party, he *really* liked to party.

The Professor frowned. "Of course not, lad. We need to toast future mutual and overlapping interests. Unless you're too good to toast with ol' Father O'Banion?"

Shay shot Brownstone a glance, confused. She'd been told before that Smite-Williams liked to go by that name, but she still had no clue what the implications were. The ignorance needled her.

"It's kind of a drinking thing," Brownstone explained. "Mostly harmless."

As long as he gives me good intel and pays me, he can get fucking plastered every night for all I care.

Father O'Banion shook his head. "Not *kind of*. It's *totally* a drinking thing, and never harmless."

He grinned as the waitress returned with the three huge glasses on her tray. She handed one to each person at the table before heading back to the bar.

The older man hefted his glass. "To defeating evil, acquiring knowledge, and making money—all at the same time."

That was a toast Shay could get behind.

"Hear, hear." She clinked her glass against his.

Brownstone only grunted before offering his glass.

Father O'Banion sucked down a good half of his drink in the blink of an eye.

Bet this guy has some artifact he uses to protect his liver.

Shay sat quietly, her gaze roaming the bar and taking in every detail. She didn't like spending too much time at a place she hadn't scoped out. She had no idea who the regulars were, so she didn't know who to be suspicious of. Just because the Professor liked the place didn't mean it was safe, and it didn't guarantee a hitman wouldn't kick in the door and put a bullet in her head.

The more time I spend out of the country, the better.

Shay considered that for a few minutes while the men drank in silence. If she wanted to really disappear, it might make sense to leave the United States and move to some tiny village tucked away into the corner of a country or island most people had never heard of.

Is that what I want? What was the point of faking my own

death if I'm just gonna run away? It's not so crazy to want a few friends who won't try and kill you if the price is right.

A life. That's what Shay wanted. After ten years of swimming in nothing but death and blood, she wanted to experience what actual life was, but that required a plan, and only the highest and broadest parts of that plan had come into focus.

That's what I get for deciding to convince everyone someone killed me without thinking it through long-term.

It didn't matter. Shay knew her eventual goal, settling down and enjoying life, her version of it. The details could be worked out in the coming months. Whatever those details were, they'd all require money, and tomb raiding would be a good way to make that cash and satisfy her love of history.

"So, you been doing field archaeology long?" Brownstone said, breaking the silence. He took a sip of his beer.

Shay narrowed her eyes, uncertain if Brownstone somehow picked up on the fact that she was new to the field. Given the way he reacted when he sat down, it was obvious the Professor hadn't clued him in about her beforehand, which meant the bounty hunter didn't have time for a background check.

"Why do you want to know? You think I don't have what it takes?"

"Play nice, children," Father O'Banion ordered.

"Nah, I know you have what it takes." Brownstone shrugged.

Shay blinked several times before her face twisted up in confusion. It sounded like a compliment, but it also implied he knew more about her than felt comfortable. They were about to go on a tomb raid that could involve them running into blood Warlocks. She didn't trust him implicitly, and she didn't get why he seemingly did.

"You *know* I have what it takes, Brownstone?"

"Yeah, that's what I said, last time I checked."

Shay almost snorted at a thought. Brownstone hadn't commented on her appearance earlier because he thought he could earn her favor a different way.

The corner of Shay's mouth turned up. "And why are you so sure? You quick to trust, Brownstone? I would have thought a bounty hunter would be more cynical."

Father O'Banion let out a quiet chuckle but didn't say anything.

"Oh, I'm cynical as any other idiot out there, but Father O'Banion wouldn't have recommended you if you weren't. I trust his judgment. I've worked with him a lot and he's never steered me wrong, which is more than I can say for a lot of people I've worked with."

Shay watched the man for a second, looking for any sign of deception on his face. His explanation again made sense, even if it disappointed her on a personal level.

Father O'Banion exhaled loudly. "Aye, lad, but all this work talk is boring."

Shay sneaked a glance his way, wondering if Smite-Williams was trying to cover for Brownstone somehow. She didn't say anything. Despite her distrust of the partner being forced on her, she didn't want to give him too much of a reason to probe her background.

"What do you want to talk about, then?" Brownstone asked.

Father O'Banion tapped the side of his glass. "Let's sit here and get drunk and tell lies. Or is that tell lies until we're drunk? Either would be fine. Both are much more fun than talking about who's a cynical fuck."

Brownstone grinned. "Can't disagree with that."

Shay scoffed. "Takes all kinds."

"That it does, but he's a lot like you."

Shay eyed the bounty hunter. "Not complaining too much. He's getting me this job, but what do you mean?"

"His appearance is deceiving."

It was like Brownstone was fucking with her on purpose, acting like he didn't have a clue one moment, and then the next talking as if he could see through her all the way to her soul. She didn't know whether to respect him or tell him to shut the hell up.

Father O'Banion nodded gravely, a ridiculously serious look now fixed on his face.

Shay's eyes narrowed, and she pursed her lips. "Oh, and you think you know me well enough to say that my appearance is deceiving, Brownstone?"

The waitress returned with another draught for Father O'Banion.

"You're doing the Lord's work, miss," O'Banion offered as the waitress departed.

The men didn't press the conversation, more interested in the beer, and Shay was more than happy to let the discussion dry up.

The more she thought about what Brownstone had said, the more it kindled a fire inside. Her old instincts kicked in. She thought over every comment the bounty hunter made since starting the conversation, becoming more convinced with each second the man was trying to make some point about her background and career choices.

Shay took a few more sips of her drink. "Look, I know what I'm doing by freelancing with my archaeology skills."

Is he judging me? He's a bounty hunter, not some priest. He needs to get over himself.

Brownstone waved a hand in front of him. "Never said you didn't."

"We all need to make our money somehow, and there's a lot of good money in artifacts. Better I make some money and steer them into someone like Smite-Williams' hands."

"Again, not disagreeing," he replied.

"She's skilled, lad." Father O'Banion's face was becoming flushed and puffy. "*Very* skilled. More skilled than a lot of people with twice her experience. Kind of like you that way."

Shay nodded. "I'm fucking Lara Croft, just without all the money. I'm doing this shit backward. Not all that interested in talking about my past, though, just in case you're the curious and nosey sort, Brownstone."

Brownstone set his glass down and nodded, no hint of defiance on his face. "I *can* be a curious and nosey sort, but I know when to leave well enough alone."

He had to go and make a comment like that.

The man will be a problem. Shay knew it. The Professor might trust him, but that didn't mean she would, not until he gave her a reason. *Trust no one and verify.*

Father O'Banion snorted. "Some people and organizations may disagree."

"Yeah, what can I say?" Brownstone said. "Results may vary. And I don't give a shit about Shay's past."

Shay gave a curt nod, glad that he was letting the matter drop for the moment, but she'd need to be careful. She sensed something in Brownstone that she recognized in herself. *The hunting instinct.*

Father O'Banion stood. "I'll be right back. Need to make more room." Whistling, he got up and wandered toward the men's bathroom.

"The past is shit," Brownstone said after thirty seconds of silence.

At least the people who took you in gave a shit, Brownstone. You don't have any idea of what it was like to grow up like I did. To start killing as young as I did.

Shay snickered. "The past is shit?"

No openings. That's what she needed to remember. She couldn't let the man gain any real insight into her past. It'd be a weapon he could wield against her.

"Yeah." Brownstone stared down into his glass. "That's what the last twenty years have taught everybody, I figure. If they haven't learned that lesson, they are dumbasses."

There was one thing she was curious about. Brownstone wasn't the meathead she thought he was, but that didn't mean he gave a shit about anything. A few probes in that direction wouldn't hurt.

Shay nodded slowly. "I get it. I mean, we all grew up reading about history and science, and what could happen and couldn't—and then we find out it's all bullshit, and that magic is real. In a sense, everything we've known… the truths humanity's known and told each other for thousands of years were all lies."

"Makes you wonder what that means for the future. There's still so much we don't know about Oriceran, and it's changing everything over here. I see it every day on my job. Fuck, that's why every country needs bounty hunters like me now."

Shay watched him for a moment, wondering if Brownstone thought of himself more as a do-gooder of justice than a simple man doing a job for money. If so, they might have problems even if he did trust her skills as much he'd claimed.

"Take the pyramids, for instance," Brownstone offered. "Big-ass tombs for long-dead pharaohs? Not even fucking close." He shrugged. "Well, okay, some were, but most of them were energy machines built by real Atlanteans hell-bent on maintaining power over twenty-fucking-thousand years ago. All that bullshit about how many years mankind has been smart?" He tapped his head. "Makes no damned sense when we have stone villages under the water in the Mediterranean Sea that are a lot older. And that lie was being questioned *before* the Oricerans showed up. Makes you wonder *who* was hiding the truth in plain fucking sight for so long, and why."

"You truly are a world-class cynic."

"I am," Brownstone agreed.

Shay managed not to grin, even though she wanted to. A cynical attitude was one thing in life she could appreciate.

She tapped her fingers against the table. "Who knew?"

"Who knew what?"

"That you *actually* had something interesting to say,

Brownstone. I kind of pegged you just as a give-a-punch-and-take-a-punch guy. That, and a grunter."

"I'm all that, too." He grunted.

Shay chuckled. The guy wouldn't be totally obnoxious. She could hope.

3

The first leg of their trip had been a comfortable jet ride down to Tapachula, Mexico. The second stage involved a smaller rickety turboprop to Peru.

Shay tried to get some rest, but it was hard in the cramped and often shaking plane. Faint tension lined Brownstone's face and had been since they'd stepped onto the first plane. He didn't say much other than some background on his bounty hunter procedures, and she didn't press the issue. She didn't want to really get into anything personal.

She also appreciated that he didn't make a big deal of her kicking the ass of a man who groped her shortly after they'd finished up their main chat at the pub. That meant, at minimum, he didn't want to try to keep her on a leash. *Smart move.*

Brownstone was there because the Professor insisted. It wasn't as if she *needed* to get to know the man. They'd spend a couple of days together, and then she wouldn't have to see him again for months, if ever.

That was the way things looked like they were playing out. *Simple.* Which is why Brownstone surprised Shay when he suddenly decided to talk about an hour into their second flight.

"What's your deal?" the bounty hunter asked.

Shay glanced his way. "My deal?"

"Yeah. The Professor hasn't mentioned you before, which means you're probably new in town. Otherwise, he would have hired my ass to be your protection a long time ago."

Shay's face twitched. She kept wanting to underestimate Brownstone, but she'd already mistaken being laconic with being an idiot at the pub. The man might not say much, but he paid attention to a lot of small details. That made him *dangerous.*

His take on history also showed that he was a bigger-picture man than she would have suspected.

Accepting that, though, made irritation flare in Shay for a different reason. She'd noticed the man, but he didn't seem to notice or care about her.

It wasn't as if she demanded or wanted every man to hit on her or anything, but Shay had as much confidence in her appearance as she did her killing skills, and that made the bounty hunter's blasé reaction a puzzle that poked at her mind.

He's gay. That works, might even be easier. That would explain why Captain Muscles didn't seem to notice her.

Brownstone kept staring at her, obviously waiting for a response.

Shay shrugged. "Whatever happened to the past being shit?"

"It is shit. But you might know more about me than I know about you."

"Nothing's different just because we're on a plane instead of a bar. I don't do bios on tomb raids, Brownstone."

The bounty hunter gave her a slow nod then looked the opposite way. "Fair enough. We can talk about barbecue if you want."

"Huh?"

"Barbecue. Do you have a favorite style?"

Shay stared at him for a moment. *Is he screwing with me or is he serious?*

"Barbecue? What the hell?"

Brownstone shrugged. "I like barbecue. I figured talking about barbecue isn't like talking about your past."

"Okay, sure. I'm gonna try and get some rest." She turned the opposite way and leaned back into her seat.

"Suit yourself."

Brownstone didn't try and follow up, allowing Shay some small peace. Every conversation with the man left her more off-balance, unlike when she dealt with Peyton.

She might spar a bit with Peyton in conversation, but she never felt like she didn't understand what was going on in his head. He was easy to read and the rest he had a habit of blurting out, anyway.

Shay kept herself from sighing. In the close quarters, Brownstone would notice.

Shay had no problems with lying to others, but never wanted to lie to herself. Brownstone got under her skin because he was messing with her life plan, even it wasn't the most detailed.

Shay was supposed to build a rep as a tomb raider, save up a fortune, and if she made it that far, move away, or hell, buy an island, and disappear.

Noticing someone wasn't in the plan, let alone someone like Brownstone.

This isn't anything important. It's just me being confused because some guy who is gay didn't comment on my looks. Simple as that.

They'd made it.

The jeep rumbled down the dirt track, bouncing and shaking the entire time. While they didn't have the luxury of taking a true road to the dig site, they'd managed to find an abandoned logging path that would get them close. After so many hours on a cramped plane, a few hours in a jeep driving through rough terrain felt like heaven.

Shay didn't care, as long as they got to the site. Finding the Rod of Supay would make her a lot more money and burnish her tomb-raiding reputation.

All her concerns about everything else, let alone Brownstone vanished before the good feeling she'd get from completing the job.

Colorful plants and animals passed in a blur, mostly ignored by the treasure hunter and the bounty hunter. They were more concerned about their mission than sightseeing.

Brownstone stared into the jungle as if he expected the Warlocks to burst through the brush at any second.

Shit, for all we know they will. Shay's focus wasn't on fighting and hunting every crazed rogue magical group out there. That was the big guy's job.

She'd brought him because the Professor made it part of the deal, but she could admit that after some of her recent close calls having a large man with a lot of guns watching her back wasn't the worst thing in the world.

Brownstone had barely spoken since they'd gotten into the jeep, not that he'd spoken a lot the entire time she'd known him. The guy liked to deliver a few smart-ass remarks, then retreat into watchful silence. *Pushing back against his conversation attempts on the plane probably didn't help.*

Being this close together only reinforced in her mind that James was probably gay. The bastard hadn't made one move on her the entire time. She had to appreciate how meticulous he was with his equipment. She shared the same attention to detail.

The silence was starting to get to her. It was one thing if she were by herself but having the man so close and not saying anything was forcing her attention away from the job. *Get over it Shay.* If he wanted to talk about barbecue now, she wouldn't mind.

"You know, Brownstone, you could talk," Shay said.

"I don't know how. Sometimes I forget."

Haha. Very funny, Brownstone.

Shay shrugged. "This might end up being pretty boring and not profitable for you if your boys don't show up."

Brownstone peered into the jungle ahead. "Oh, they'll show up."

"How can you be so sure?"

"The bait's too great, and the Professor wouldn't have bothered asking me to come if he didn't think you needed me."

It'll be interesting to see what three Warlocks can bring. Snegurka times three would have been damned hard to win against by myself. But both of us should be able to take them down easily.

"That's a comforting thought."

Brownstone grinned. "Well, I'm not here to make you feel better. I'm here to take out any bastards that bother us."

Shay slowed the jeep as a large mound in the distance caught her eye. "Looks like we're almost there."

The only problem was the trees thickening ahead of them. *Where was a clear-cut when you needed it?*

They both fell back into silence and searched the area for any signs of recent passage. From what Brownstone had told Shay on the first leg of their plane trip, the Red Warlocks specialized in blood magic. At least they wouldn't have to worry about a fireball exploding over them out of nowhere or ice lances.

Shay frowned and brought the jeep to a stop. "We'll have to hoof it from here. Too bad. A few miles in the jungle isn't a recreational hike."

Brownstone moved his head back and forth, popping his neck. "Then we'd better get going."

4

They got out of the jeep and hiked through the jungle, finally coming to stand in front of a crumbling stone archway and weathered stairs leading into inky darkness below. Torn small flags and the occasional discarded tool hinted at the last group of explorers.

Shay glanced around the area, taking in the details. It wasn't underwater. That was a plus.

"Not a lot of climbing involved." Shay linked her fingers and stretched her arms above her. She double-checked her holster, her machete sheath, and her knife sheath.

"Sure."

The noise of the jungle surrounded them. The flutter of birds' wings, buzzing of insects, the shuffling of unknown beasts.

Shay glanced around, looking for any sign of the Warlocks. That kind of men getting their hands on the Rod of Supay would make for a huge mess. *I might be here to make money, but nobody needs a zombie rod getting into general circulation. There goes the neighborhood, forever.*

The tomb site lay atop a tall cliff with a river snaking past well below it. The site was inaccessible from that side because of the difficulty of scaling a cliff in the middle of dense jungle, but in an emergency, they could probably climb down and follow the river.

They approached the stone arch, and after exchanging glances, they pulled out their flashlights and turned them on. The beams cut into the darkness, revealing nothing but stairs descending to a dusty chamber below.

"Let's do this." Shay felt a calm come over even as the thrill of the hunt came over her.

Brownstone nodded.

Their footsteps echoed in the eerie silence until they arrived at the bottom of the stairs, where smaller tunnels branched off in three directions. Their equal spacing around the room made them hard to differentiate. Shay could see how someone could easily get disoriented in the chamber.

She was ready. She'd paid close attention to her angle as they entered the chamber and knew exactly where to go.

The treasure hunter pointed to her left. "That leads to the main burial chamber. Given the small size of this place, I think it'll be easy to find the rod." She stepped toward the tunnel.

"Glad *some* things in life are easy."

Shay grinned. "This place has mostly been excavated already, so we don't have to worry about traps or anything until we get near the main burial chamber." She grinned, the shadows of the tomb giving her face a sinister visage.

Excitement swelled in Shay.

For all the talk of the creepy Warlocks, she might be able to snag the artifact without much trouble in the end. Getting a payday would be sweet enough, but being able to do it without breaking a sweat?

That was a big-assed bonus.

Shay chuckled to herself, thinking about Brownstone as their footsteps echoed and mingled in the narrow passageway. Even though the gay bounty hunter insisted he had nothing but respect for her skill, he probably still carried some doubts. Recovering this artifact would prove to him that she had what it took, and then…

Then what? Shay furrowed her brow. It wasn't like the man was going to eat his words. He'd already said that he trusted in her skills. She gritted her teeth. It was frustrating when she was ready for a fight, but the other person wouldn't play.

Damn it, Brownstone. Be less frustrating and more openly annoying.

Shay shook it off and focused on the job.

Brownstone walked beside her in silence, step after step. The sound was hypnotic when she focused on it.

It took her a few moments to accept what she was hearing. A strange buzzing that had not been there before. She was sure of it.

In any other place, the slightest background noise would have swallowed the buzzing. Birds tweeting or the slight rustle of the wind would have been more than enough to mask it, but there in the shadows of the tomb with nothing but the eternal silence of death, the quiet sound stood out as if someone were screaming.

Shay's heart rate kicked up and she froze in place for a moment, slowly turning around, her hand dropping to the holster. Taking a slow, even breath, she pulled her weapon out.

Brownstone had already drawn his pistol. "You heard it too. I'm impressed," he whispered.

Shay arched an eyebrow, ignoring the comment and peered into the darkness, holding her flashlight arm under her pistol arm to help better steady both. Her beam joined the bounty hunter's in piercing the darkness.

We're close to something.

It didn't take long to find another anomaly. Her beam caught a faint shimmer near the entrance, just past where they'd entered the tunnel. Her partner's beam caught something that made her let out a hiss.

Brownstone changed his angle toward the floor while Shay illuminated the shimmer. Bloody footsteps marred the floor.

The shimmer vanished, and three men in scarlet robes winked into sight.

"If you leave now, you won't die. You cannot defeat the *Brujos Rojos*. Your greed has brought you to your doom." The figure spoke in a deep voice that echoed in the space.

"Okay, that confirms we found the bad guys," Shay muttered. A little clarity always made things a lot easier.

Brownstone holstered his pistol. "Yeah, I'd worry a lot more about your own doom there, assholes."

"What the hell are you doing?" Shay whispered. "Are you planning to *talk* them into submission?"

Brownstone chuckled. "If only that would work." The bounty hunter shook his head, even as he kept his gaze locked on the three men. He spoke in a whisper. "I've dealt with the *Brujos Rojos* before. They like to get close. If they can get a good cut on you, their blood magic is fucking vicious."

"Isn't that more of a reason to shoot them from *very* far away?" *What is the line between confident and cocky?*

"Nope." He shrugged. "Go ahead and take a shot."

Shay frowned. The men's threat had made their identity clear, and even if they were willing to let Shay and her support go, they'd get control of the zombie rod. She wasn't about to lose her payday and let some asshole Warlocks get a free artifact. She pulled the trigger.

One of them men jerked, and Shay waited for the payoff and a groan, followed by a body drop. She had plenty of confidence in her weapons skills, and it was satisfying to see a bad guy go down.

Except that he didn't. The struck warlock remained silent as he dropped his robe to the ground and pointed to the new, large wound on his shoulder. Even though his face was contorted in pain, the flesh was already repairing itself.

"Something about soul proximity or some shit." Brownstone kept his focus on the Warlocks. "Overly complicated crap. All I know is that they are dangerous up close, but they are also weak up close. And if they are out cold, their magic is worthless."

Brownstone sprang at them suddenly, surprising Shay. The Warlocks recoiled, just as surprised. Their fingernails grew into glistening claws as the charging bounty hunter had already closed the gap.

He slammed a fist into the head of the closest warlock,

crashing him into a wall with an echoing thud before he fell to the hard stone that paved the floor of the tunnel. Taking advantage of his momentum, he landed a spinning kick square on the chest of a second warlock. The man smashed headfirst into the tunnel wall opposite the first warlock.

Brownstone grinned. Shay didn't mind. *There's nothing wrong with enjoying your work.* It's not like she didn't get satisfaction out of taking a mark down in her old job.

The only remaining warlock was Shay's bullet sponge.

His wound had already sealed itself.

The bastard offered James a sickening grin. He'd taken the time to cast a spell while his friends were getting the beat-down. A bloody film now covered the warlock's eyes, and they glowed with a soft crimson light.

His newly-grown claws dripped with a dark liquid.

Shay slammed her pistol into her holster and unsheathed her knife. She didn't want to let Brownstone show her up, but she didn't have to be an expert mage to recognize that the warlock was sporting poison-tipped claws. The power of blood magic couldn't be easily dismissed.

Brownstone stared at the man for a second before shaking his head. "Still not too late to surrender, asshole."

Apparently, Brownstone was a little less impressed. If he ended up getting his ass wasted, it wouldn't be her fault. Walking the line between confident and idiotic could be difficult.

The warlock yelled and slashed at the bounty hunter, as he grabbed the man's arms and yanked hard to either side, dislocating both the man's shoulders. A blood-curdling scream filled the chamber. Brownstone finished by head-butting the warlock's face, and the man's nose crunched, as his eyes rolled up. The bounty hunter let go, and the unconscious man fell to the ground.

Shay caught up to James. "Okay then, Brownstone, I'll admit it. You've got skills."

Her background check of Brownstone, along with his class five status, meant he'd be able to handle this sort of thing, but all that information was just bytes in a computer and rumors in the end. Seeing the man take down three Warlocks like he was going out for a jog crystalized the truth of his skills in her mind.

He jerked his thumb at the other end of the tunnel. "You go get the Rod. I'll deal with these jokers."

Shay nodded and jogged back the way she'd come, her heart still racing from the short fight. She didn't expect the Warlocks would be too much trouble between the two of them, but at least a *little* bit of a problem. James' presence was a bonus… even if she was going to keep that to herself.

The tunnel gave way to an octagonal room. A large stone sarcophagus dominated the center, its lid already removed by the previous expedition and its occupant was also gone.

Shay didn't care. She wasn't there for a dead Incan. She was there for a rod that made dead people rise up and walk. She circled the chamber, carefully pointing her flash-light at the junctures where the walls met the floor. Her research told her there was a hidden area in the room.

A couple of minutes' effort rewarded her search, although she would have missed it if she hadn't known exactly what she was looking for. It was a small carving in the wall that from a certain angle, illuminated with only a single beam of light resembled a stylized humanoid figure.

The earlier expedition might have eventually found it if they didn't have to worry about things like Communist insurgents. Shay smiled. When she'd taken the job, she wasn't worried about the idea they might run into local rebels. Brownstone didn't seem to care either. The only real threat were the Warlocks.

Of course, even if the earlier expedition hadn't fled, they wouldn't have found what she sought. The Professor had told her the magical shielding of the site had concealed hidden treasure chambers like the one she was about to open.

There was probably gold and jewelry to be found, but she didn't care. The payoff from the Rod made the trip worthwhile, and she didn't want to stick around in case more Warlocks showed up. Handling thirty might not be as easy as handling three.

Even if the expedition had found the spot on the wall, she doubted they would have been able to figure what to do next. Being a *field archaeologist*, whether you wanted to call someone in that profession a treasure hunter or tomb raider, required equal parts daring and knowledge.

Blood freely given will reveal the sacred treasure. Shay grabbed her knife and sliced the tip of one of her fingers. Rubbing her hand over the carving, she grinned to herself.

I'm damn good.

The burial chamber rumbled, and Shay straightened, crossing her arms and waiting. The wall parted on the other side, revealing a small stone box and a faded wall painting of a dark-eyed man in a dark cloak wearing a round golden headpiece. She'd seen similar depictions in her research for the job.

It was undoubtedly Supay.

Shay searched around the box for any indications of a trap. Satisfied that she wasn't about to be blown up or poisoned, she pushed the lid off, releasing a cloud of dust.

A curved bone rod lay inside. Swirling patterns and sigils that Shay didn't recognize decorated the artifact.

Not taking any chances, Shay slipped on gloves before grabbing the Rod of Supay. Fortunately, from everything she'd read, it didn't activate without exposure to blood. She slipped the covered rod into her backpack and took a deep breath.

"That went well."

She had to admit that if she'd been by herself, she might have misjudged the Warlocks, but that didn't mean they would have won. It wasn't that she *needed* Brownstone.

He'd just made things easier.

With the Rod of Supay in hand, Shay didn't see any reason to stick around. She walked quickly out of the burial chamber and headed into the tunnel. Brownstone was gone, as were the downed Warlocks. Picking up the pace, Shay hurried out of the tunnel into the entrance chamber and up the stairs.

The bounty hunter stood at the top, an unconscious and zip-tied warlock lying next to him.

Shay patted her backpack. "I got it."

"Good."

She glanced down at the warlock. "What happened to the other two guys? When we were flying down here, I thought you told me that you could get a bounty per guy."

He shrugged. "No room on the plane. I should have thought that through." He pointed his thumb over his shoulder. "I threw the other two into the river. Hope the alligators don't get indigestion."

Shay stared at him for a moment. He looked bored, and she had no idea if he was telling the truth. *For all I know, he ate them for magical power. We need to get out of here. I'm rolling with this one.*

"You have a very dry sense of humor, Mr. Brownstone," Shay told him. "Let's get the hell out of here."

5

S hay smiled to herself as she stepped out of her red Fiat Spider and walked across the campus to the modern Fielding building where she lectured, named for the late President.

She'd already delivered the Rod of Supay to the Professor. Brownstone hadn't been there. He was off turning in his bounty.

She didn't know what to make of the man. He frustrated her on many levels, but at the same time when it came to the job he was an efficient professional, and that's something she could appreciate.

That didn't mean she wanted to work with him all the time, but the whole thing hadn't turned into the disaster she'd expected.

Working on the right side of the law will allow me to learn to trust people a little bit more. Just...

Time to switch gears a little and get into her role as professor. Still, she couldn't stop herself from scanning the different clusters of students and professors all hurrying off to a class or sitting on nearby benches.

Not a bad impulse to keep. Getting lazy about surroundings is how even a retired hitman gets herself killed.

Shay adjusted the satchel in her hand containing her notes, and a small throwing knife in the side pocket just in case, and quickly strode up the wide steps, taking them easily in her three-inch heels.

She got to the lecture hall, the rows where the students sat rising up in front of her and put down her belongings. The room was already filling up, students eagerly taking up the front rows. Shay gave a cool glance around, inwardly pleased that the word was spreading across the campus. This was a hot academic ticket.

She glanced at her phone and saw a text from Peyton to pick up more flour and some *good* coffee, arching her eyebrow and tucking the phone into her bag. *Useful annoyances can wait an hour.*

Shay glanced up at the large clock at the back of the room, perfectly situated so only she could see it without craning a neck. "Okay, everyone settle down. Time to start. Someone please close the doors at the back." Shay already had a reputation for stopping the class whenever someone came in late, silently waiting till they took their seat before picking up the lecture again. The same was true if anyone tried to duck out early.

No one dared to make either move. It didn't matter, the topics kept everyone interested and Shay was able to give such details it was like the students were there. It helped that some of the time, Shay was there.

"Recently a group of two-thousand-year-old skeletons were found at the foot of a massive coal-fired power station in Kostolac, in north-eastern Serbia. They were discovered on the site of what was an ancient Roman city, Viminacium. Remember, the borders of Rome stretched far and wide in those days, aided we now know by magic."

There was a murmur through the crowd and Shay looked around, waiting till the slight buzz of chatter calmed down.

"Found grasped in each hand of one skeleton were two small lead amulets." Shay showed a picture of them on the virtual screen behind her. She had taken the pictures herself before carefully locking the amulets away in one of her warehouses. The picture showed two amulets, both three inches long, one more circular than the other.

"Inside of the rounder amulet was a two inch by three-inch rectangle of thin gold metal with ancient Aramaic inscribed on it. Inside the other amulet was a similar silver sheet with more Aramaic inscriptions. Both are ancient spells forgotten to the past till now."

And locked up safely in my vault where no one can use them.

"In the past we would have written off the idea of magic as the way ancient civilizations explained things they didn't understand. As it turns out, we called the existence of magic bunk as a way to explain what we feared."

A hand shot up from a curly-haired freshman who Shay recognized from the girl's stops by her office on campus. "Yes, Sandy?"

"Did they discover what kind of spells?" The words came tumbling out of her.

"Two thousand years ago all spells were called, binding

spells, whether they were for good or to cause harm. The spell attached an intended outcome to someone to fall in love, or to drop dead right where they stood. These particular spells were to keep the dead from coming back, and this case... again."

Other evidence had told Shay the ancient wizard was good at bringing himself back to life. "The dead man was believed to have been a powerful Oriceran who was defeated in a battle that raged between the two worlds." And then came back to life to turn the tide, putting Earth at risk. Others prevailed at the cost of some of their own lives, silencing him for two thousand years with two small curses.

Shay had gone on the trip with instructions from a wizard who liked playing fast and loose with the law but had managed to stay away from any bounty hunter, so far. She had traded him a minor artifact with limited powers for the details of how to make the dead stay dead, and still be able to grab the prize.

They started with a blazing bonfire and a carefully whispered spell that turned the flames blue. She carried his bones to the fire, placing them on top with his bony hands outstretched toward Shay. At the last moment she snatched the artifacts out of his clutches and watched in awe as he briefly came to life, his bones momentarily taking on flesh only to realize he was in a trap that he wasn't going to escape this time.

Shay had let out a deep breath of relief, even as she waited till all the fire had died down and prepared to bury the ashes, repeating the spell just as she was told to do. "Skip nothing," the wizard had said, tapping the side of his long, broken nose. "The success of your operation will be in the details."

The ashes swirled around her as she repeated the spell, the artifacts carefully tucked in her bag, sucked into the hole at her feet as she whispered the last words. *Zayin Peh.* Sword ends.

Shay told the entire story to the rapt students replacing herself in the adventure with an unknown Serbian scientist who had supposedly related the entire story to her. She showed pictures of the tiny metallic scrolls and the burned ground where the fire had burned such a vivid blue. "Sometimes when you bury the past, you had better shoot it first."

Not a bad life, she thought, noticing the hour was winding down. *As long as the different pieces never meet.*

Shay finally pulled into Warehouse Two, the roll door slowly closing behind her. Peyton emerged from the maze of cubicle walls that marked the pop-up apartment he'd set up inside the warehouse. He was wearing docksiders and navy-blue pants with a cross-stitched belt of sailing flags that spelled out his name, and a white t-shirt.

"Relax, I'm moving out soon."

"To a boathouse?"

"So funny. This was a hot look in the eighties. I can see the tension all over your face. I'm not moving *all* your things around."

"Don't remind me. When do I get to see this new place and make sure it's secure?"

"When you find it… Okay, okay, that was too soon. I don't have the keys yet, but I'll take you as soon as I do. Hell, you can help me move." Peyton gave a helpful shrug as Shay shook her head.

He had already proven his usefulness, and Shay trusted the man as far as she could shoot him, which was progress. But their shared secrets helped to keep the calm between them, too.

"Hey," Shay said. "I just got the big payday."

"Found the zombie rod, huh? Congrats." Peyton grinned. "What was Brownstone like?"

"Confusing, and pretty badass."

Some of Peyton's grin faded. "I take it you did run into trouble on the job?" He rubbed his wrist.

Shay gave a short nod. "Sure did, three blood Warlocks, but Brownstone took them down like they were old ladies. It was damn impressive."

"Huh, you should…"

"No." She held up a finger to punctuate her sentence.

Peyton blinked. "You didn't even hear what I was going to say."

"I *know* what you're gonna say. I worked with the man for one job. I respect his skills, *but* the last thing I need to do is get dependent on other people. That's dangerous."

"Work with other people? You mean like certain research experts?" Peyton patted his chest with his hands. "Or am I just special?"

Shay shook her head. "That's different. We have an understanding. I can't necessarily trust Brownstone. He wasn't there to help me, not really. He was there to get some bounties."

"The enemy of my enemy is my friend, right?"

"No, sometimes the enemy of my enemy is just another enemy." She shrugged. "More people means more things to go wrong, and if Brownstone knew the truth, he'd probably try to get some sort of bounty set up for me. I wasn't exactly a saint in my old life."

"He only goes after the magical kind of bounties. I get it, it's a no go." Peyton looked disappointed. "Just seems like a waste."

Shay frowned. Spending more time around Brownstone was a bad idea. She got into this business to make her own way. Not take on a partner.

Need to take care of Peyton's dead man's switch sooner than later too. Get rid of all the entanglements.

"I don't want to worry about Brownstone. Let's go out to celebrate. There's a pizza place I don't usually go to except for special occasions. Might as well introduce it to you now."

A look of confusion settled over Peyton's face. "None of your other jobs were special enough to celebrate?"

"They were special, but this is kind of a milestone. Smite-Williams represents top-tier jobs. We're now officially in the *big leagues.*"

"True enough. I'm surprised there's a pizza place you haven't taken me to yet. Not going to complain though."

Shay nodded toward her Fiat. "Get in. Let's go."

Shay smiled to herself as they stepped inside Dante's. She loved the understated elegance of the pizzeria. Dark earth tones dominated the booths and tables. The delicious scents of the spices permeated the air. Her mouth already watered, and her stomach rumbled.

The current owner, Andrew, offered her a nod as she entered, and an eager waitress hurried over with a smile on her face.

"The usual, ma'am?" she asked.

"Sure." Shay nodded at Peyton. "For both of us."

The waitress led Shay and Peyton over to a booth in a corner that provided a clear view of all the exits and windows without her back being exposed to a shooter. She couldn't always get the booth, but none of the other customers, mostly older men in dark suits, occupied a table or booth close to her favorite spot.

A lucky day after a good job. She wasn't going to question it.

"I'll be back in a moment with your wine, ma'am," the waitress said. She looked over at Peyton. "And you, sir?"

"I'll have what's she having." He shot Shay an uncertain glance.

"Of course, sir." The waitress scurried off.

Peyton leaned over the table, his gaze searching the rest of the tables. "This is Dante's," he whispered. "*The* Dante's."

Shay laughed. "Yeah, I know. I'm the one who brought us here."

"And they know you. You have a *usual*, which means you come here more often than special occasions, but you've never mentioned coming here before."

Shay shrugged. "So sue me. I had a life before I saved yours, you know."

Peyton slowly turned his head around, taking in the

other patrons as he took in deep, long breaths. *Be cool.* "You do realize there's several big-name mobsters sitting in this place right now?"

"Yeah, I do." Shay tilted her head, offering a hint of a smile to Peyton. "Time for a little test. Show me how much you've learned about L.A. Explain to me why this place is special other than just the connected guys sitting around us."

Peyton sighed and glanced over at a nearby booth. "This place is kind of known for being popular with the older L.A. gangsters. According to the rumors I've heard, early meetings here twenty years ago helped birth the local dark magic underworld in L.A. You know, the kind of people that make people like Brownstone necessary. This is not a safe place. Far fucking from it."

"Give the boy a gold star." Shay smiled as the waitress arrived with their bottle of wine and filled their glasses.

"Your food will be here soon, ma'am." The waitress hurried to another table.

Shay waited until the woman was on the other side of the room to speak. "That's the good thing about having you as an assistant. I don't have to waste time explaining shit to you. You've got initiative and a thirst for knowledge. I really appreciate that."

"Even though you regularly threaten me with a bullet hole or two?"

"What can I say? It's a complicated relationship with no 401k necessary."

Peyton glanced around the room again, tension lining his face. "I haven't heard anything to suggest this place isn't still a popular dark magic underworld hangout."

Shay took a sip of her wine, enjoying the fruity notes of her Chianti. "Neither have I, and like you pointed out, there are several mobsters here, and some of these people I don't recognize. Who knows who they might be? Mobsters? Magical killers? Lots of possibilities. Kind of exciting when you think about it."

"Are you insane?" Peyton whispered, his face growing pale.

I'm pushing him a little hard, but he's gonna have to learn not to get spun up by this sort of thing. At least I've almost got him cured of his Chicago-style pizza shit.

"Not last time I checked, ignoring the whole going after dangerous magical artifacts for a living thing." Shay nodded toward his glass. "Drink a glass of wine and calm down. This place isn't a big deal, and it has good wine."

Peyton rolled his eyes as he took a sip. "Okay. I'll admit it. It is good wine, and I'm not even that much of a wine guy."

"See?"

"But that doesn't change the fact that we're sitting in a place where some magical assassin could show up any minute. You're good, but you don't have magic."

"Messing with Dante's is just going to cause them trouble. But sure, somebody really dangerous could pop in. They could fireball this place before I even knew what the fuck was happening."

"Why are we here then?" Peyton swallowed and lowered his face even more. "Isn't this way more dangerous than me going to the store? Or even getting my own place. I can't let my guard down long enough to take a bite."

Shay took another small sip of wine. "You can't let your

guard down anywhere. Here, you never forget, and some-times the best way to stay alive is to remind yourself not to get complacent. That's why I love coming here, and I'm always more relaxed overall than I am most places."

The waitress arrived with their thin-crust pepperoni pizza.

Shay and Peyton fell into a more comfortable silence as they attacked the pizza.

"Bet this place is near a warehouse," Peyton mumbled through a full mouth. "That probably explains the real deal."

Shay shot a grin at him. "Chew, swallow, repeat... not. You'll have to try and find that out yourself."

"It is good pizza, though." A lot of Peyton's color was returning. "Very damned good. Wonder if they use magic when they cook it."

"Only the magic of a great woodfired oven."

Peyton's eyes widened. "I've just had a great idea. Fantastic idea."

"What? Tomorrow you're going to wear a yellow suit and start carrying an overly curious monkey around with you?"

"No, I mean... huh? Whatever. No, you love pizza, and you're rolling in the dough, metaphorically at least. We should put in a pizza oven in... the place I live." Peyton glanced around for a moment, suspicion on his face.

Shay appreciated his situational awareness, though she didn't worry about anyone keying in on references to warehouses. The average customer in the room probably had warehouses containing something far worse than equipment and weapons.

"I don't even have a pizza oven at home," she said. "So why would I give you one?"

Peyton blinked. "You don't? You, Queen of all Pizza?"

"Nope."

"Why not?"

"Because there's a lot more to pizza than the oven. Besides, I thought you liked going out."

Peyton nodded. "I do. Was just a thought."

Either Peyton was adjusting to the situation or his wine was kicking in. His shoulders had loosened, and the lingering concern in his eyes vanished.

He downed half his glass in one gulp. "Speaking of me getting out. It won't be the end of the world if I lived in an actual apartment. Look how easy it was to bring me here."

"Yeah, you're right but we need to be smart about it. Do what you do."

"What do you mean?"

"Research it, Peyton. Make sure you've looked at it from all the angles. I have just as much interest in making sure you don't make a mistake picking a place, so I'm reserving a veto, once I see it."

Peyton polished off his wine. "Fair enough."

Shay's phone buzzed. "One sec."

Bella was texting her.

Hey, girl. You interested in doing something in the next few days?

Sure. Just let me know.

Okay, going to text the others.

Peyton glanced at the phone. "Trouble?"

"Far from it. Just trying to arrange a girls' night."

Shay allowed herself a smile. She led two different lives, both completely compartmentalized. She liked it that way.

When she'd worked as a killer for hire, there was no other life around so much death. Her friends were people involved in the scene, one way or another. Now, though, she could have fun when she didn't want to worry about zombie rods, blood magic, or barbecue-loving muscle-bound bounty hunters.

L.A. granted a person freedom, as long as they wanted to maintain a false front. It was the perfect place for that, the capital at the heart of an Empire of Masks. She fit right in.

Peyton poured himself a new glass of wine. "So there's something I've been wondering. And I wanted to kind of ask about it."

"Yeah? What?"

"You're making a lot of money."

Shay shrugged. "Not a big secret from you."

Peyton frowned. "It's just... what are you even planning to do with all that money? It's not like you're saving up for any reason. If you kept your head down and lived a real quiet life, got rid of your warehouses, you could probably live fine for a while."

Shay shook her head. "I can never assume that I'll have a truly quiet life. If I try to go be a soccer mom in Wyoming, eventually someone will catch up to me unless I have the resources to see them coming and deal with them. Even then, a lot of people around me might get hurt."

"So that's what all the money's about? Protection from your past?"

Shay locked eyes with Peyton. She could tell him about

her plan to go move to another country or buy an island, but she had no real details to share, and even if she trusted him more than she did yesterday, sometimes it was best to not let him know how much she was making up as she went along.

Confidence was important in getting people to trust you. If you didn't have it, you might as well fake it.

"Long-term plans are for suckers," Shay said. "Tomorrow I might be dead or teleported to some Oriceran swamp."

Peyton stared into his wine. "Cheerful thought. I'm going to keep assuming I'm going to live and plan accordingly. If someone kills me early, well, it won't matter that it messed up my plans because I'll be dead."

Shay gave a dark chuckle. "True enough. You never know, you could get lucky and come back to haunt their asses."

6

Shay's phone blared a harsh tone, jolting her out of her carb-induced deep sleep. A few seconds passed till she remembered she was at her condo. She shook her head to clear it before grabbing the phone.

Everything was going too well. I should have expected something like this.

She killed the alarm and checked the security feeds. The muffled crack of automatic rifle and pistol fire reached her ears.

A regular person might have thought they heard car noises or something else, but Shay recognized the weapon fire and likely scenario without any trouble, even some of the weapons being used. Someone was going to town with some AKs and pistols.

Her heart rate kicked up, and she took a deep breath as she went over her evidence. Her security set-up wasn't limited to her home, and the weapons fire was obviously not coming from inside or being fired at the condo based on the noise. She wasn't under attack, but whatever was going on was close and involved more than a couple of gangbangers shooting at each other with .22s.

Fucking perfect. Just fucking perfect.

Her security feeds revealed armed men pouring into a home a few buildings down. Several black SUVs lined the street.

Shay let out a long groan. "Are you kidding me? I just got done dealing with Warlocks and zombie rods, and now this shit?"

Judging by the lack of obvious gang colors and the weapons, Shay figured out it was a cartel raid. She was aware of a stash house down the street but didn't care. If anything, she'd figured the presence of such a juicy and obvious target would shield her own presence from attention, even if she was renting the place under a false name.

Yeah, not surprised, but doesn't mean I'm happy, either. Hiding next to the blindingly bright target didn't work out as well as I wanted. File that under failed experiments.

Shay adjusted her cameras to get a better angle on some of the assault force. She flipped on the night-vision mode and ran the faces of the men she could get a clear view of through a facial recognition algorithm that fed into data sources Peyton helped her set up. Maybe she'd get lucky and could figure out who had showed up to play.

Her stomach knotted as several names popped up linked to the Nuevo Gulf Cartel. That was attention she didn't need, especially since those men wanted her dead, and she'd killed several of them recently.

Technically, they already thought she was dead, and she didn't want to do anything to disabuse them of that notion.

Should just let the assholes shoot it out. It's not my business if

*one group of assholes gets butchered by another group. The cops
will come soon, or some bounty hunter like Brownstone.*

*Now that would be funny. I'd like to see what we could do to
the sicarios out there.*

Shay furrowed her brow at another thought. It wasn't
like she was the only one who could use technology to
disrupt communications. There might not be anyone on
their way to deal with this mess. The bloody raid might
play out in its entirety, with the authorities not investi-
gating until the next day.

Damn it. Is this gonna get worse before it gets better?

Even if the raiding party was using some sort of
jammer, it still didn't mean she needed to get involved.
One side would win, and it still wouldn't be her problem.
There was no innocent blood getting spilled over in that
house, just scum gutting scum. In a sense, they were both
doing the world a favor.

Several of the men who'd entered the house burst out.
One clutched his side. They fired rounds into the house as
they ran down the sidewalk in the direction of Shay's
condo, passing by another home. The raid wasn't going as
well as they hoped.

"Of course. Damn it. No one's good at their fucking job
anymore."

Shay sighed and threw off her nightgown, replacing it
with some shorts and a tank-top. So much for staying out
of it, and she wasn't about to paint her nightgown red with
the blood of the Nuevo Gulf Cartel.

She pushed a false wall in her closet to the side to grab
her emergency tactical harness. It already held a Glock, a
few spare mags, and several knives.

Luck was where opportunity met preparation, which is why Shay never, ever let herself be unprepared.

Thanks for really ruining my night, assholes.

Most of the raiding party remained inside the stash house, but she wasn't sure if they were pushing back against the enemy inside or dead. None of that stopped the five men who leapt over her fence into her backyard.

Okay, now you've stepped in it.

Shay grumbled as she raced down the stairs, skipping a few steps at the bottom. She tossed her phone on the end table, drew her gun, and rushed into her kitchen as one of the cartel members jiggled her door handle. The bastards wanted somewhere to hide. They could have gone in any direction, or even screwed with the house right next door, but they had to choose her house. *Big mistake*, and the last they would ever make.

I'm gonna provide a little service to the neighborhood. Too bad no one will ever know.

Shay ducked behind her island, holstered her weapon, and readied a knife instead. Killing them with a minimum number of gunshots lowered the chance of attracting police attention. She couldn't rely on idiots who'd screwed up their own surprise raid to keep the authorities away. She slid another knife into her open hand.

There is absolutely no fucking way I'm letting these assholes kill me in my kitchen. I'm not Natalie, and I don't give one shit about the universe's sense of irony.

A loud bang sounded, and her door flew open.

"No alarm," a man said in Spanish. "Too trusting. I'm going to head upstairs and finish anyone off before they call the cops."

"You do that," another man responded.

"Anyone coming from the stash house?"

"Not that I can see. I think we lost them."

The first man grunted. "The boss will be mad."

"Better than being dead."

Shay held her breath and crept to the edge of the island. Small flat green lights in a few of the light sockets pushed away total darkness in the kitchen and allowed Shay to spot the shadow of a large man skulking into her kitchen.

Should have stayed in the stash house. It's a lot safer there, assholes. Now get ready for a real killer.

Shay leapt up from behind her island. She didn't even give the first cartel member time to do more than let out a surprised grunt before slashing his neck open. A quick spin ended with her second knife in his partner's throat.

Yeah, better than being dead, indeed.

She yanked out the blade, and the man gurgled and collapsed to the ground, blood spraying from his neck.

The three remaining men backed away from the door and squeezed off rounds. Shay dodged, but a stray bullet struck her knife blade. The blade snapped in a shower of sparks, and the two halves clattered against her kitchen floor.

"Damn it," she mumbled. "That was one of my favorite knives."

Shay returned the other knife to its sheath and pulled her gun back out. She wouldn't be able to close on her enemies now. The cartel members peppered the kitchen with gunfire, but their panic led to them not wounding anything but walls.

You assholes are almost embarrassing.

This group only had pistols, rather than the rifles. A bullet storm from five AKs on full auto might have been too much even for Shay to dodge.

She darted across the kitchen toward the living room. Bullets followed her path.

"Come on, assholes. Take the bait." Shay crouched near her stairs, her gun pointed at the kitchen door.

True pros wouldn't come into the living room. They would spread out and flank her on both sides of the house. But these panicky fools had tried a home invasion after running away from a failed raid. Right now, they possessed the tactical acumen of rabbits high on cocaine.

Everything I've heard about the Nuevo Gulf Cartel getting weakened by competitors is true. Or these guys were always pussies waiting for someone to stand up to them.

Shay didn't have to wait long. Heavy footsteps filled the kitchen, and a few seconds later, the first man entered the living room, his gun up.

A single round between the eyes brought him down. Shay put three rounds through the wall right next to the door. A man yelled, and a loud thump followed. She sprinted toward the kitchen and jumped in, twisting sideways.

The final cartel member waiting on the other end of the kitchen didn't even get time to pull the trigger before Shay shot him. She hit the ground before he did.

Shay hopped to her feet and put a few more bullets into the downed men. She headed over to the back door and closed it.

Five dead bodies and several bullet holes in the walls. Not exactly the least suspicious gathering of evidence, even if the most gullible cop or cartel member showed up to check out what happened.

Damn it. Why did these guys have to pick my house?

A heavy sigh followed. Five cartel members ended up in her house. It'd been a coincidence, and the lack of sirens suggested at least someone was directing the cops away from the incident for the moment, but it didn't matter.

Someone would investigate, either criminal or cop, and they'd stumble on her place and then it wouldn't be a stretch to figure out that the name on the lease didn't go with the woman inside, especially since she'd proven she could kill five cartel enforcers.

"Damn it. it's a warehouse for the night."

The condo served her well, and some fondness might remain in the coming years as she thought about her place in L.A., but for now, she needed to burn any connection she had with the place.

Time to fucking go.

Luck, as mediated by preparation, was again on her side.

Shay headed back into the living room and grabbed her phone. She scrolled down her contacts list and dialed.

"Purity Solutions," a cheerful woman answered. "Your 24/7 cleaning and moving solution."

An always open firm might be suspicious, but it wasn't like people not in the know even had the phone number for the company. She needed her place cleaned out without a trace of even DNA ASAP, and that wasn't something she could manage alone, or even with Peyton's help.

"I need to confirm an emergency spring cleaning and

move," Shay said. "There are... moderate complications involved."

From what she remembered of their briefing when she put down her deposit, moderate complications including things like dead bodies. Severe complications covered a room filled with dismembered corpses. Even Shay shuddered at the kind of person who needed that cleaned up quickly.

"Do you have a confirmation number, ma'am?"

And here I always thought it was silly to have memorized it, but I've been paying for this.

"KLZ255842," Shay related.

"Ah, ma'am. I see you have a prepaid service account. Any particular details you'd like to share about the nature of the cleaning and move that would be helpful for our staff to know?"

"Two-bedroom condo." Shay rattled off the address. She wandered into the kitchen to glance at the bodies. "Need everything prepped for an immediate move. Also some minor wall touch-ups and garbage disposal."

"Of course, ma'am. What sort of touch-ups?"

"Just a few holes filled in the wall from nails."

"I see," the woman said, her voice still as cheerful as ever. "Would these be large nails, small nails, or medium-sized nails?"

Shay glanced at one of the bullet holes, uncertain as to Purity's exact standards when it came to bullet sizes.

"Medium-sized. Just normal wear and tear from an active lifestyle and a party I just had. Not a huge number of people at the party."

"Sure thing, ma'am. Our staff will be able to quickly take care of those. And the garbage you mentioned?"

Shay sighed. "Just some old clothes that needed to be taken care of. Five garment bags worth. All the clothes are still together, though."

"Okay, ma'am. We can have someone over in about twenty minutes to take care of the garbage. The rest will be taken care of by the end of the day, and you can contact us about delivery. It's best if you're not present once our staff arrives, as it cuts down on misunderstandings. Thank you for using Purity Solutions."

Shay ended the call and sighed. She didn't like not cleaning up her own messes, but she needed to get the hell away from everything that had just happened.

Time to pack a few things and get out of here. It's a good thing I had that two-story brownstone already lined up.

7

Shay pulled her red Fiat Spider to the curb at Brownstone's house. She wasn't even sure why she'd bothered to come. Maybe some part of her wanted to confirm that the man was gay so she could explain why he hadn't made any moves. So she could stop thinking about *him*. Checking out his house would help her gather evidence.

On the other hand, if Brownstone *wasn't* gay, he might make a pass at her in a more comfortable setting.

She also wanted him to know she could take care of herself. It's not like he'd said she couldn't, but the idea that he was sitting around thinking that she needed him to watch her ass annoyed her.

It'd help for Shay to get to know the bounty hunter better anyway. She didn't have to, or even want to, be his friend, but it would help when working together on future jobs. The more in sync they were, the better the chance they'd both come out of it alive and richer.

You're useful, Brownstone, but you're not indispensable. Just a hunky tool.

Whatever the treasure hunter thought about Brownstone's personality, she acknowledged that he was a first-class fearless ass-kicker and a good guy to have on your side in a fight. Warlocks weren't normally so easily killed. If they were, the world would be a lot safer.

Shay threw open her Fiat's door and stepped out. She walked to Brownstone's front door and knocked several times. No answer. She repeated the process with no greater success.

"Are you even here?" Shay grumbled. That was what she got for not bothering to call ahead. For all she knew Brownstone was out drinking with Smite-Williams or getting laid.

A light breeze blew, and an all-too familiar metallic scent reached her nose.

Shay's heart rate grew steady and calm as she slid her gun out of her shoulder holster. It was always better to be overly cautious. She lacked the nose of a shifter, but she'd been around enough bloody messes to easily recognize even a faint whiff.

After a quick check of the nearby area, Shay hugged the wall and made her way to the corner of the house. The breeze brought the smell again. It was coming from a source outside the house. The lack of an obvious body in the front told her the body she presumed she would find lay out back. She reached the corner and took a deep breath.

Gun raised, she whipped around the corner. No

enemies or gunfire greeted her—only silence and an empty side yard.

Don't be dead, Brownstone. No man who can kill three Warlocks like that should get taken out like a bitch at his own house.

Careful steps brought her into the backyard.

A small cardboard cross caught Shay's attention. It stood atop the disturbed soil of a freshly-dug grave, another sight she was distressingly familiar with.

Shay slipped her gun back into her holster and peered down at the grave. The cardboard wouldn't last long, and the grave was too new. All signs pointed to a recent burial, if not that day.

"Leeroy" was the sole word on the cross.

The dog.

James had talked about him briefly during their time on the planes. It was one of the few times the guy had seemed normal to her; even pleasant. Another gust blew and the cardboard swayed in the wind, revealing more writing on the back.

"Remember," Shay read. Kanji characters had been printed next to the English word. "Oh, shit."

Shay didn't know Japanese, but she did know the Japanese characters for Harriken.

"It's got nothing to do with me," Shay muttered to herself. "It's not..." She sighed, her palm going to her forehead. "That's just low, Harriken. Too damn low."

Killing someone who had it coming was one thing. Hell, killing someone who didn't have it coming but could at least defend themselves was justifiable—depending on the circumstances—but killing some poor dog who didn't have a chance was over the line. The kind of men who did that had no limits.

The treasure hunter swallowed. She knew about people with no limits. She used to be one. Maybe still was.

Shay knelt and found a large rock. She pulled out her knife and scratched Leeroy's name, the current year, and "You will be avenged" underneath. She wished she knew what year the dog had been born so she could add it to the stone. Maybe she'd ask Brownstone the next time she saw him, if he'd not gotten himself killed already.

"Damn it." Shay stood and walked back toward her Spider. Leeroy's death had nothing to do with her, but that didn't mean she was going to let Brownstone get himself killed. She had a pretty good idea where he would be partying that night.

A sick smirk grew on her face. The good thing about the Harriken being such arrogant douchebags was that they didn't hide much. They didn't think they had anything to fear. Anyone in Los Angeles with an ounce of street knowledge knew the location of their headquarters.

"Am I really going to do this?" Shay muttered to herself. She started the car. "Fuck it. I was bored anyway." She slammed down the accelerator and peeled out.

Shay's initial plan had been to do a quick recon of the house; just a simple drive-by to check out the number of guards out front. That plan ended the second she spotted the two downed Harriken guards near the front of the house. The broken and cracked front door lying on the lawn made it clear that Brownstone had already begun his revenge assault.

"Subtle," Shay muttered.

Still, she could admire the direct approach. Killing someone should be an up-close and personal affair. If you didn't get a little blood on you, you were being a pussy.

Of course, charging in the front door was its own special form of moronic. A smarter play would have been to go around the back or climb up the side for a second-story entry. Strolling in the entrance went past moronic to downright insane.

At least for most men. Brownstone had proven once again that he wasn't like most men. Not even close.

During the entire drive over, Shay had kept trying to tell herself that it wasn't her business. It had nothing to do with field archaeology. Nothing to do with her.

Still, somehow she'd convinced herself to drive halfway across town to attack Harriken headquarters and help avenge the murder of the dog of a guy she didn't even like that much.

Plus, the man didn't give her a second look.

You better damn well be gay, Brownstone. Frustrating didn't even begin to describe the situation. Idiotically frustrating, maybe.

"What the hell am I doing?" Shay ran her hands through her dark hair and sighed.

Brownstone was already inside, and the angry fool might need her help. If she didn't help him out, the next person who ended up in a shallow grave might be her. The Harriken might go after all the bounty hunter's associates.

The assholes had murdered a dog. It wasn't like she

could be assured that there was no photo of her standing beside her recent partner. The Harriken were thorough when they felt they had been disrespected.

Self-preservation served as a nice excuse for Shay to help. It was time to get involved.

Shay parked along the street and rolled her window down. She waited for thirty seconds, listening for the sounds of closing sirens. She didn't want to tangle with a deploying SWAT team. Shooting at criminal scum was one thing, pissing off the authorities quite another.

The last thing she needed was for anyone to go digging into her past. She'd worked too hard to escape it.

Not even a hint of approaching cops reached her ears. Even the nearest cars sounded far away.

It was just a nice, quiet little neighborhood street where a man was engaged in the bloody revenge-fueled massacre of a ruthless criminal gang.

If that didn't scream *AMERICA!*, nothing did.

The neighbors probably knew not to get involved in Harriken business, and the cops might have been paid to look the other way. In either event, the circumstances granted her what she needed most. Time to check things out.

Taking a look inside didn't mean she was committing to dying in order to pull Brownstone out of his own shit.

After a quick pat of her holster and sheath, Shay threw the car door open and stepped outside.

"I'm as stupid as Brownstone," she muttered to herself, drawing her gun. "Not even gonna make any money off this shit."

Shay rushed toward the house in a zigzag pattern.

Assuming the entire enemy force had been completely devastated might get her killed. For all she knew, Brownstone was bleeding out inside, and a Harriken sniper was aiming down his sights and waiting for reinforcements to pick off. Helpful reinforcements like her.

The frustrated field archaeologist's arrival at the front door remained uncontested. No sniper blew her head off.

Nice night so far.

The front door more closely resembled a front *hole.* Two Harriken enforcers lay on the ground. One man's head hung at an unnatural angle, and his head and face were smashed in from what looked like extreme blunt-force trauma.

Shay eyed the body with clinical detachment, wondering if Brownstone's punches could do that kind of damage. Whether or not they could, the even and wide bruising patterns didn't support that theory. Something else had killed the man.

What kind of weapon did you use, Brownstone? Did you show up with a shovel or something?

Killing the men with the shovel he had used to bury his dog would be poetic. And badass.

Her gaze traveled to the hole and to the cracked and bloodstained door lying on the lawn. Her eyes widened.

No, not a shovel.

"What the fuck?" Shay whispered.

Did you seriously use a guy as a battering ram, Brownstone? I don't know if I'm impressed or fucking terrified. Must be a little of both.

The other bloodied man's face remained intact, which was probably why he could still let out a quiet moan. Shay jerked her gun toward the man, but quickly realized he wasn't a threat. His mangled buddy would need a closed-casket funeral.

Shay squatted next to the guy and considered her options. Taking him out would be easy enough, but she sensed that Brownstone wanted the guy alive for some reason. There was no way the bounty hunter wouldn't have finished the Harriken off otherwise. Brownstone had broken down a door using a man's body. Restraint in the application of violence didn't seem to be one of his virtues.

Gonna interrogate this bastard later, Brownstone? Is that the idea? Should have pinned a note on his back so I didn't waste my time.

The Harriken moaned again.

"It's either your lucky day," Shay began, "or the worst fucking day of your life. You'll find out later." She kicked him hard in the head to knock him out again.

A charnel house awaited Shay inside. Bodies littered the crimson-soaked floor and stairs and blood dripped a slow and steady beat to the floor from some of the corpses on the stairs, a metronome of carnage. One poor fucker was half-embedded in the wall like some bizarre wall decoration.

Salvador Dali meets Ed Gein.

"Jesus, Brownstone. How did you even get him through there?"

No pity pricked her heart for the dead Harriken. They'd pissed off the wrong man, and now they were paying the price. Any halfway decent criminal organization knew who to poke and who to leave alone. She hoped whoever was responsible for Harriken intelligence was lying in this room or on the stairs.

Organized crime was like any other business. Cost and benefit needed to balance, and the executive committee meeting on this fuckup was something she would pay big money to listen to.

Shay swept the room and a few other connected rooms, her gun ready, but spotted no active enemies. She headed back into the front room. The walls on the opposite side were perforated with dozens of jagged holes, some small, some large.

It's a goddamn warzone.

The treasure hunter took a few steps forward, looking down at the bodies on the floor. She didn't lower her gun. One surprise Harriken ambush and she could end up dead.

Shay furrowed her brow and thought about every piece of evidence she'd seen so far.

Let's see... No shell casings outside. The guards' guns hadn't even been drawn, which meant they hadn't shot. Brownstone must have walked right up, and they had probably talked some shit back and forth. Didn't use anything but his hands, most likely.

The big guy entered through the front after bashing it open with a Harriken guy's body. Killed these guys on the floor. No gun, all knives and fists. Damn could that guy hit hard. What the hell was he?

Shay blinked and looked up at the large dent in the ceiling.

Seriously, Brownstone? How did you hit a guy all the way up there?

The fight in Peru had taken place in too small a space

and over too short a time span for her to witness Brownstone's true strength. She exhaled slowly, glad that the guy seemed calm most of the time. She could only imagine what would happen if he decided to go from being merely an asshole to a murderous asshole.

Shay's focus shifted back and forth between the bodies and the bullet-riddled walls. Brownstone had obviously used the walls for cover. She doubted the shooters had engaged him until after the first wave of men had died at his hands.

That made sense. The Harriken must have banked on the men on the first floor outnumbering their enemy, but sometimes quantity *didn't* have a quality all its own.

Shay didn't spot any throwing knives in the stair bodies. Large holes marked the bodies, mostly around the chest. She walked to the bottom of the stairs and rolled one of the bodies over. Smaller entry wound in the front, bigger exit wound in the back—she'd seen that before.

Brownstone took cover behind the swiss cheese walls of death there and started taking these guys out...with what? Probably a large-caliber pistol with hollow-points. This wasn't just defense. He wanted to make sure he took the guys down. Definitely not trying to take a lot of prisoners. Also meant that Brownstone didn't think he was going to have to shoot through a lot of walls.

Shay chewed on that thought for a few seconds. Brownstone had assaulted the headquarters, motivated by vengeance. He might have wanted to see his enemies die in front of him.

Not unexpected.

She padded toward the dining room, keeping her gun ready. No bloodstains or bodies presented themselves on the floor, but .45-caliber brass shell casings lay all over. She performed a quick count.

Had to change mags at least once in here. Probably only once, though.

A small amount of blood stained a side wall. Shay looked between the hole-pocked walls and the wall with blood, aiming her gun to help her visualize the line of fire.

Brownstone took a hit. Not enough to take him down, obviously.

Closer inspection of the wall led Shay to spot a small bullet hole.

He took a hit, but the bullet passed clean through. Good for him, and lucky the Harriken *weren't using hollow-points too.*

Shay shook her head as she headed back toward the stairs. Violence was an art in and of itself, and the gory scene at the house proved that Brownstone was the fucking Jackson Pollock of ass-kicking.

A few quiet moans sounded from the stairs. Shay rushed into the front room, hurrying behind a couch, gun drawn. A sprint to a chair followed. No Harriken popped up to shoot at her as she approached the source of the moans. Two survivors.

Sloppy, Brownstone. Then again, these guys are obviously gonna bleed out.

"Help...me," one of the men groaned. "Can...pay...you. Earn...respect of the...Harriken."

"Yeah, about that...First, I just got a big paycheck today, so I'm not as impressed with money. Second, it doesn't make much sense to help out the guys who got their asses kicked and piss off the guy who did the ass-kicking. Sorry."

Shay tossed her pistol into her other hand and yanked out her knife, as she walked to the man, pulled his head up, and slit his throat. The other moaner met his end right after. A quick check of the other bodies confirmed no more survivors, but she sliced their throats to be certain.

Stray thoughts about the Rod of Supay filtered into her head, and Shay resisted the urge to head-shoot all the corpses. Not only would it waste ammo, but she wasn't even sure that worked on zombies in real life.

Keeping her gun ready, the woman crept up the stairs and along the wall—more like a member of the SAS than a field archaeologist. She swept into each room, ready to shoot at any target presenting himself.

Each upstairs room stood empty, except for one containing a dead man with a katana beside him and a huge puncture wound in his throat. Shay stared at a bullet-riddled door lying against the wall opposite the open doorway.

Okay. Brownstone thought someone might be hiding, and he opened up on the door—or maybe he was just trying to see something. Why the knife? Downstairs showed that he's got good aim. Not a single sloppy shot in the bunch, and he was under fire probably the whole time.

Shay furrowed her brow as she tried to piece the clues together.

Katana guy must have gotten the drop on him, otherwise Brownstone would have put a bullet into his head or chest. Or three bullets.

From the look of things, this guy was high-ranking.

Harriken *do place a lot of importance in personal ass-kicking ability. Maybe Topknot Boy knocked Brownstone's gun out of his hand?*

She spoke to the corpse. "You probably thought you had him, didn't you?" Shay snickered.

She crept out of the room, pointing her gun downward as she approached the stairs. There was only one major area left to explore, and that lay behind the reinforced door to what she assumed was the basement. After a trip through the killing fields, she closed on the door.

Someone, presumably Brownstone had fired a shitload of bullets into the door to create a hole where the lock used to be. A huge pile of shell casings lay near the door, and she knelt to inspect them.

Only a few were .45s. Most were 5.45×39mm.

James opened up with what...probably an AK? Did you run in here with two guns, Brownstone, like some VR shooter sim?

No. That's not right. The fuckers on the stairs all looked like they died from pistol wounds. Probably some Harriken *guy showed up with the AK, and Brownstone took him out and used his gun as the world's bluntest lockpick.*

Shay searched around and found the expected rifle, snapped into two pieces shoved under one of the bodies. Brownstone was covering his back.

A full picture of the assault crystalized in her mind. Brownstone hadn't approached the headquarters with anything resembling stealth. Had never planned to. He'd boldly walked right up, knocked a guy out, and beat his partner to death in the process of using the man as a living battering ram.

Well, semi-living.

Outnumbered and outgunned, the bounty hunter had executed all his enemies while taking only a hit or two.

All because these men had killed his dog.

James Brownstone was a living bulldozer crossed with a tank designed in Hell.

Shay shook her head as she processed it all. The fight against the Warlocks hadn't demonstrated one-tenth of this lethality. Anyone picking a fight with Brownstone should schedule their funeral ahead of time to save their relatives the trouble.

A couple of *thuds* sounded from downstairs, and Shay nodded to herself. Brownstone didn't need her assistance. The death tableau had proved that.

I can still walk away. The Emperor of Destruction here doesn't need my help. Leeroy has been avenged, and then some.

Shay stared at the basement door and shook her head. "This is stupid." She sighed and grabbed the handle.

8

Shay crept down the stairs, only to run into more of the aftermath of Hurricane Brownstone. The bottom of the stairwell led to a short corridor that turned to the right before joining a larger hallway. With the cement walls and stairwell, Brownstone would have been fed straight into a kill box.

Except he wasn't the one who was dead.

A dead Harriken lay against the wall, his face bruised, his eyes closed, and his nose askew. His sword had been driven right through his chest. Another man lay on the floor facedown, a pistol a few feet from his hand. His sword remained in its sheath.

Several flattened bullets littered the floor. Huge chips in the cement walls let her know the man had fired his pistol and missed his target.

Shay began to wonder how these final men could have believed they'd even have a chance against Brownstone. From what she could tell, they'd had fortifications and surprise...but still lost.

Maybe a few rocket launchers or some sort of powerful magic would have helped.

Brownstone's voice echoed from the other end of the basement, and Shay sidled closer to him. She holstered her gun and peeked around the corner just in time to see the bounty hunter decapitate one man and rant about barbecue to the second before punching him in the stomach.

The only surprising thing about the sight was that Brownstone's second target didn't cough up blood and fall to the ground dead.

His survival told Shay that James must have pulled his punch. After everything she'd seen in Peru and in the house that night, she didn't believe a normal human could survive such a blow. She wasn't sure what Brownstone was but she refused to believe that he wasn't relying on some sort of magic. Normal people just weren't that strong.

James kicked the pistol behind the last man.

"I...apologize to the dog," the Harriken wheezed. "Please spare me."

"He wasn't just 'the dog.' He had a name." Brownstone crossed his arms and glared down at the man. "His fucking name was Leeroy."

"Okay, okay." The Harriken lifted his hand placatingly. "His name was Leeroy."

"You don't get it. I want you to apologize to Leeroy using his name."

"But he's dead."

"And you're gonna join him soon."

The gangster managed to sit up, though one hand still rested on his stomach. A grimace seemed surgically attached to his face at this point. "But...you're really here because you want to know where she is, right?"

Brownstone crouched by the man. "I told you why I'm here. Because the Harriken murdered my dog."

"I told them not to do it. I told them we should leave you alone. I'd heard of you before."

"That's an interesting story, but even if I believed it, I don't fucking care." Brownstone scratched at an eyebrow. "You were telling me how the Harriken would grow stronger, get their vengeance on me and come after everyone I love. Don't you remember that?" He shrugged. "It wasn't exactly ages ago. I know I hit you pretty hard. Your memory may be a little fuzzy. And I seem to remember a speech implying my dog wasn't that important." He stood again. "Makes me question your honesty, fuckface."

The spectacle transfixed Shay. Whether Brownstone was offering a casual discussion of barbecue or threatening to kill the Harriken over his dog, the feral menace never left his deep, growling voice. The man's appetite for vengeance hadn't been sated, despite killing almost everyone else in the house. The purity of the brutality was as fascinating as it was unsettling. To call him a killing machine would be insufficient.

A force of nature, maybe.

"I apologize to Leeroy," the Harriken man said, now able to get his words out more steadily. "It was stupid of us to do what we did."

Brownstone snorted. "Stupid?"

The Harriken prostrated himself. "It was wrong. We disrespected you. We disrespected Leeroy." The man kept his forehead pressed against the floor. "But we know you want her, too. We know that's why you've interfered with us."

Shay furrowed her brow. Brownstone hadn't mentioned much about his previous work during their job together, though now that she thought about it, it made sense that the Harriken must have had some decent reason to come after him.

Her first thoughts went to possible Harriken bounties, but the groveling gangster's words said something more complicated. She doubted Brownstone was involved in any sort of Harriken scheme. The bounty hunter didn't strike her as the type who would play too many sides against each other.

Shay didn't doubt his intelligence. It was more that she doubted his patience.

"Interfered with you?" Brownstone repeated. "It's more like when I go somewhere, you assholes show up and cause trouble for me." He let out a weary sigh. "And that first time, I was just trying to pay a favor back for someone who helped me find my dog. You see how that works? You help me with my dog, I help you. You kill my dog, I kill you. Fucking simple, right?"

The man on the ground swallowed, but didn't respond.

"Your first two guys could have turned around and left. Or you guys could have never come to my house. Or killed my dog." Brownstone shrugged. "If you'd refrained from doing that I wouldn't have gotten in your face. I wouldn't have had to kill any of you, just like I didn't kill those first two assholes. Fuck, I don't give a shit about bounties on small fry like you. It's not worth my time. Right now, I'm just trying to decide if I need two guys running around telling people why they shouldn't go after me, or only one. 'Cause I got one guy already upstairs still alive."

Shay nodded to herself. She'd been wrong about why Brownstone wanted the man alive, but she'd been smart not to kill him.

The gangster raised his head, his mouth pressed into a thin line. It was a hard thing to stare death right in the face. The man was used to being on the other end of this kind of exchange.

Some might call it karma in action.

Brownstone didn't really care that much about bounty money. His skills meant he could have easily made a lot of cash if he were willing to help the right kind of corrupt people. An enforcer who could tear apart a house filled with armed men would be a useful weapon for plenty of organized crime groups, let alone terrorist groups, rogue nations, and God knew what sort of weirdos from Oriceran. In the chaos of the current world, it was smart to collect all the weapons you could.

Killing some blood-magic Warlocks in a narrow tunnel was one thing, but the assault on the Harriken headquarters proved that Brownstone wasn't remotely allergic to violence and didn't need self-defense as an excuse to kill.

Money couldn't be a big motivation for him, but then... The pieces didn't fit together, and Shay felt like she was missing something.

Shay resisted a sigh. She didn't want to alert Brownstone to her presence.

She'd seen enough. The bounty hunter obviously didn't need her help, and he could finish up with the remaining

Harriken man without her spying on him. She stepped around the corner and crept back up the stairs, the sound of the conversation fading into the distance.

Shay leaned against her Spider with her arms crossed. She'd thought about leaving but wanted Brownstone to know she'd at least bothered to show up. Even if she didn't play well with others that didn't mean Shay didn't understand the importance of building trust.

Brownstone emerged from the house and glanced down at the Harriken Shay had knocked out earlier before looking at her. She gave him a quick, casual wave and waited for him to walk over to her.

"You're about the last person I expected to see here," Brownstone told her when he reached her. Weariness infused his voice, not unexpected after annihilating an entire house full of hardened killers.

Shay shrugged. "I wanted to talk to you, so I stopped by your house."

"And?"

"I got suspicious and poked around. I thought something had happened to you, and then I found Leeroy's grave. I'm sorry, Brownstone. You got dealt a shit hand."

"And why did you come here?" he asked, blunt as usual.

"You're a useful guy to have on treasure hunts. If you're gonna die, I'd prefer it be fighting off Warlocks trying to steal zombie rods rather than random gangsters."

Brownstone grunted. "The only people who died tonight were Harriken."

Shay waved a hand dismissively. "Fair enough. Point is, I showed up and saw that everyone was dead inside. I figured you had it handled, and I didn't want to poke around in some spooky basement."

"You'll go into an Inca tomb, but a basement bothers you?"

"Funny how that works." Shay grinned.

Lying came easily and naturally to Shay, but a twinge of guilt hit her. She wasn't sure why she didn't want Brownstone to know she'd witnessed his encounter.

The bounty hunter grunted and nodded at the house. "I killed everyone in there except one guy at the door, as you know. I was going to let one more guy go, but he tried to take a shot at me."

"That was dumb."

"Yeah."

Shay stared into his eyes for a moment, looking for any sign of remorse. Failing to find that, she sought pleasure. She didn't find that either.

Brownstone had done what he needed to do to avenge his dog. Nothing more, nothing less.

Blood soaked his shirt on the side and on his shoulder. The man's t-shirt was more a shredded rag than a piece of clothing at this point.

Shay had spotted the stiffness in his movements when she was watching him in the basement. This close to him, the bullet wound was obvious.

"Do I need to take you to the hospital?" She shrugged. "Or do you use some back-alley surgeon?"

Brownstone shook his head and gingerly moved his

arm. "Bullet went clean through. I have a first-aid kit in my truck. I can just sew it up."

Shay eyed him with open disbelief. "You're tough, but you're not gonna be able to sew up your own shoulder with one hand." She sighed. "Fortunately for you, I've done this sort of thing before."

"Knew a bunch of lowlifes like me who wouldn't go to the hospital?"

"Something like that."

After shrugging the unwounded shoulder, the bounty hunter turned and started toward his truck. Shay followed him the few blocks, leaving her car where it was.

When they got to his vehicle, Brownstone pulled the first aid kit out of the backseat and a spare faded t-shirt out of the front seat.

Shay almost laughed. It was like he'd expected to survive but lose his shirt. He must wipe out large gangs on a schedule.

Maybe it was Brownstone's idea of a fun weekend.

A quip came to her lips, but it never made it out. Instead, she found her attention locked on the man's body. It wasn't that she hadn't noticed his muscles before, but with his shirt off, his rock-hard abs forced her attention despite the weeping slashes in his side and the bullet wound.

The man was the captain of Ripped Town, USA. The savant of six-packs... No, the president of Rippedtopia. Even with the ridges on his face and the odd birthmarks, she could see how a woman could be into him.

Frowning, Shay tried to push the thoughts out of her head. She wasn't interested in Brownstone that way, and even if she were, it didn't matter because the guy played for the other team. Sewing up wounds was more important than some stupid man's abs and pecs.

She forced her eyes up. "Got any topical anesthesia or anything?" After a few seconds, she added, "Maybe some magical shit?"

Curiosity propelled the question, along with a desire to probe the mysterious bounty hunter's life just a bit more. The more she learned about him, the better she'd be able to put together the puzzle of the truth behind the man.

Brownstone grunted. "I don't like magic much. I avoid it when possible."

"Oh?" Shay found the statement hard to believe but pissing him off after he'd killed a houseful of Harriken didn't have much upside for her.

"Guns and bandages are more reliable," he continued.

"Not disagreeing, Brownstone." Shay shrugged.

His choice of words struck her as very deliberate. The man was comfortable enough around magical artifacts to help out on raids for Inca zombie wands, and he'd obviously done a lot of work for the Professor. He probably had a few artifacts stashed somewhere for difficult bounties.

"Getting shot hurts a lot more than getting the wound stitched up," Brownstone muttered.

Shay pulled out some disinfectant gel, gut, and a needle from the first aid kit. Her skilled hands soon closed all the bounty hunter's wounds. His face barely moved as she pierced his skin and sutured it.

"There. Can't say you won't scar, though."

"They can join the club. Thanks for the help."

"You're welcome."

Shay stopped her finger from instinctively tracing some of the other scars on his body. Each one drew her in as a mark of the man's life-and-death struggles. A person didn't really know who they were until their life was on the line. Brownstone must have had a hell of a good idea of exactly who he was.

"Hey, you like barbecue?" the bounty hunter rumbled.

"Seriously? You're asking that now?"

"Why not?" Brownstone shrugged. "I'm hungry, and I didn't eat before coming here for my errand." He slipped on the gray t-shirt. "We're not that far from Pork Gods, and they are open late."

Shay stared at Brownstone, trying to process that the man wanted to go for some barbecue right after dishing out that bloodbath in the house.

Her stomach rumbled. A meal might be nice.

"'Pork Gods?'" Shay snickered. "They think pretty highly of themselves. But, yeah, sure, whatever."

9

The sun started to rise on Shay's drive to Warehouse Two. A new day for another new change in her life. She was less annoyed with having to move than having to do it so quickly.

This time she could genuinely say she didn't have it coming. She just happened to be in the wrong place at the wrong time.

So that's what it feels like.

Shay rolled into the building, stifling a yawn. It'd taken her ten minutes to grab what she needed, secure the secret panel and escape in her Fiat, and she assumed that Purity staff were already at her place cleaning up her mess in every sense of the word.

If I'm gonna have any sort of real plan for the future, I need to stop ending up in situations where I have to run from my house and disappear at a moment's notice after killing someone.

She let out a quiet laugh at the thought. What a fucked-up life she led. Even when she was trying to be normal, it still ended in bloodshed.

Peyton emerged from the cubicle maze, confusion on his tired face and red reindeer pajamas on his body. "Oh, good. I half-wondered if someone had shown up to kill me. It's just you."

"Not exactly moving like you were trying to stay alive?"

"If someone's going to kill me this early, then they'll probably have an easy time of it." He let out a long infectious yawn. "Seriously, what are you doing here so early?"

Shay shrugged. "I had to kill five people at my condo earlier. Don't worry, though. They all had it coming."

Peyton blinked several times, his eyes widening. "A mention of a quintuple homicide worked better than an IV drip of coffee." He swallowed. "You okay?"

"I'm fine. Like I said, I'm the one who killed them. They didn't even hit me."

"Were they... I mean did they come there for you? For your contract?" Peyton furrowed his brow. "I haven't seen anything to even suggest that the people who wanted you dead know you're still alive." He rubbed a hand over his face. "Damn it. Did I miss something? I'm sorry. Fuck, is that a firing offense, literally..."

Shay shook her head. "You did your job. They weren't there for me, not originally. The whole thing was kind of incidental. They picked the wrong house."

"Incidental? How does that happen? I mean some guys just stopped by your house, and the next thing you know five people are dead?"

"Yeah, pretty much. Men from the Nuevo Gulf Cartel raided a nearby stash house. They botched the job, and some of them tried to run. Five of them were gonna hide in my house and kill me. I objected to that. A few minutes later I had a bunch of dead bodies in my house and figured I'd better vacate the property."

Peyton groaned. "Shit. We need to get out in front of this. The cops are eventually going to investigate the raid, if they aren't already. Their cyber guys can barely catch a cold, but because the cartel's involved, they'll get the feds involved, and they might find something we don't want them to find."

He's got good instincts. Glad to see him realizing all the implications.

Shay waved a hand. "Don't worry. Purity is cleaning up the place." She blew out a long breath. "But still double-check at the end of the day that the utilities and other accounts are linked to some other fake name. Arrange a pickup of all the weapons in my place and seal up the stash room permanently. It doesn't hurt to be careful. Other than me getting a new place, this isn't a huge deal. Fucking assholes inconvenienced me is all."

"Will do." A thoughtful expression crossed Peyton's face. "People actually do use Purity?"

"What you thought the whole thing was some kind of urban legend or something?"

"No. More a scam. I mean they have a good reputation in the dark web, but the whole idea always seemed weird. If there's a need, someone will fill it."

Shay laughed. "You think a company that specialized in scamming people like me would last long? I don't exactly take my complaints to the Better Business Bureau."

"I suppose not." Peyton's eyes lit up. "Does this mean we're going to be roomies, then? It'll be like a violent summer camp or as I call it, middle school."

"I'd sooner shoot you. I was planning to move to the new place. This just gives me a reason to expedite the process." Shay yawned. "Mostly I wanted to let you know what was up. Plus, this is a little reminder of the danger of living out there, instead of here."

Peyton shrugged. "I'd still rather have my own place. I'll just avoid killing a bunch of guys in it."

Shay snickered. "You make it sound so easy. It actually wasn't my fault this time."

"I've managed to go my entire life without killing anyone. It's surprisingly easy." Peyton winked.

Shay smirked back at him, even as his words burrowed deeper than she would have liked.

Her first ever kill had been in self-defense, but she didn't continue on the path of killing because she had to, but because she liked the sense of control. Not only that, she was damned good at the job.

Killing made her feel *strong*. It was addictive.

Shay dug a dark and deep hole inside of herself, and if she wanted to claim a new life not steeped in blood and suffering, she'd have to spend some time climbing back out of that hole.

She leaned back in her chair and stared up at the light fixtures on the high ceiling.

Don't know if I deserve a second chance. Don't care, really, but the least I can do is try.

Shay wiped some sweat from her brow as she jumped from the top of her climbing wall onto the waiting bar in the salmon ladder. She pushed and jumped with the bar, the metal slamming against metal as she ascended the obstacle with ease.

An earlier confirmation message from Purity indicated her old place had been cleared out, and the utilities transferred to a fake name. Peyton also confirmed that there was nothing, at least electronically, linking Shay to the condo and the weapons were secure.

Free and clear. It was like she'd never lived at the place. Never existed.

It's a good thing I never talked to my neighbors.

Shay arrived at the top of the salmon ladder and leapt from the bar to her unstable metal balance beam. The impact of her landing stretched the bungee cords holding it up, and it swung back and forth.

No big deal. The money's been transferred, and I'll be living in that brownstone soon enough.

An image flashed in her mind, not of the two-story property, but of the muscled bounty hunter. Her foot slipped, and she fell.

Shay caught the beam with her hand and took a deep breath before letting herself fall to the ground in a controlled manner.

What the fuck?

It'd been a long time since she'd had an accident on her obstacle course, so long that she didn't bother with much in the way of mats or other safety precautions. Training when you knew you had a second chance ended up training you to be sloppy. Real risk promoted real skills.

Why the hell did I suddenly think of him? That's not like me. Just because of the name?

Shay jogged back toward the climbing wall marking the start of her course. Brownstone the man wasn't important, and she didn't want him to set up shop in her head.

True, he was the first man she'd found intriguing in a long while, but that was because he acted like he didn't care, and she was more than comfortable explaining that away as the man being gay.

Unless my gaydar is broken... Is that all I need? A local non-sassy gay friend who can kill three Warlocks like he does it every day?

Hell, for all Shay knew, Brownstone did just that.

Being a solo killer before provided a certain elegant simplicity to her entire existence.

Friends, lovers, neighbors. All were distractions. That's what she'd believed for most of her life. Opening herself to another seemed like a fatal mistake. The only person anyone could rely on was themselves.

And what did thinking like that get me? Killing a friend in my kitchen.

Shay shook her head and grabbed a handhold on the climbing wall, a dark chuckle escaping her mouth. *Starting over...*

Life was just like the obstacle course. She could never accomplish anything real emotionally if she never risked injury.

———

"Two unannounced visits in one day," Peyton said as Shay emerged from her car into Warehouse Two. "I'm honored."

Shay shrugged. "It is my building. It wasn't always your house... or apartment or whatever you want to call it."

"Sure, sure. Please tell me you didn't come to check my work personally. I know what I'm doing. You have to know that by now."

"Your work? You mean looking into my utilities transfer? Nah. I'm confident enough in Purity, and I know that kind of thing is kindergarten shit for you. Is that what you want to hear?"

Peyton shrugged. "It is nice to hear in between the snark and threats."

Shay marched into the cubicle maze and what amounted to Peyton's living room and slipped into a chair. "This is about something else entirely."

"Kill someone else on your way here? Let me guess. You had no choice?"

Shay laughed. "Not that I'm aware of. I was thinking earlier, and I figured it was about time I started taking advantage of some of your special skills."

Peyton dropped into an open lounge chair. "I'm flattered, but aren't you already doing that? Isn't that the whole reason you saved my life, rather than my stunning fashion sense?"

"I come to work just to see what you're wearing. It's not your computer skills, your magical research skills, and not just for tomb raid shit. For equipment."

The man's face brightened. "Oh?"

"Yeah. During my little disagreement with the cartel, my favorite knife snapped."

"Sorry to hear that."

"Well, it got me thinking. Why does a knife have to break?"

Peyton extended the footrest on his chair, and put his legs up "Because everything breaks eventually?"

"Not everything. We're just used to it as a human civilization, but there are plenty of legends about unbreakable weapons out there, which means there must be magic that can accomplish it."

"Okay, I'm following you. I think. You want an unbreakable knife?"

"Yeah, a few knives that are always sharp, light-weight, and don't break. If I'm gonna be playing with other people who are using magic, I need to start using it to my advantage, but in ways that I can easily control as a normal person." Shay shrugged. "I'm not asking for Excalibur or the ability to cut through steel or anything. Just knives I can stab a cartel guy in the throat with and not worry about them breaking."

"Normal business meeting. I can hang with this."

Shay threw a pillow at his head as Peyton easily ducked. "This is our normal."

Peyton nodded slowly, his brows knitted together. "You're in luck. I think I know a guy."

Shay jerked forward. "You know a guy who can make unbreakable knives?"

"Well, I know *of* a guy. Guy's not the right word. I know a Gnome. Not sure if they like being called guys or not."

"Where did you find this guy, Gnome, whatever? Did you find him on Yelp?"

Peyton looked away. "Not exactly."

"Not exactly? Care to clarify that. This is only my life on the line."

"It's not like I literally went to Yelp, but even on the dark web there are ratings *if* you know where to look. And I basically found some pieces of information on dark magic on the dark web."

Shay peered at Peyton with suspicion. "And you just happened to already know what I was looking for before I knew it? You're a psychic and a hacker now?"

"I've become good at reading you. It's a gift." Peyton hooked his fingers in his belt and grinned. "Something like that. I've already been researching this sort of thing because I thought it'd come up sooner than later. This guy comes highly rated and should be perfect for what you're asking. I want to prove my skills as much as you want to use them, you know."

Shay was impressed and dismayed at Peyton's ability to predict what she'd need. Perfect for an assistant. Dangerous for a tomb raider. She smiled at him, one eyebrow arched. "Thanks, Peyton. That's damned helpful."

He bent over at the waist, sweeping his arm out to the side in a bow from his seat. "I live to serve. One little thing though..."

"What?"

"It's kind of hard to find his place."

"How hard could it be?"

It is damn hard to find this place. Of course. It's magic.

Shay hopped off the escalator. Her search of the first floor of the old mall netted nothing but annoyance and frustration. She passed the Yankee Candle store again, a waft of a mixture of strong flowery scents hitting her in the face.

Onto the second floor... The Gnome's shop is in here somewhere. That much I know for sure.

Peyton said his shop was located in the mall, but he couldn't give a more specific location than that. She needed to examine each shop and concentrate on the idea of finding the Gnome's shop if she were to have any hope of locating it. There was some sort of protective spell on it.

Yeah, this isn't fucking annoying at all. This goes well beyond just not having a web site, asshole.

Shay passed the CVS and stopped, doubling back. In the window were small, wind up toys floating midway up the window, walking on air. *Magic...* Shay took a deep breath and let her shoulders relax. *Be the Gnome. Fuck, that's not it. Find the Gnome.*

Nothing. Shay tried it again but still nothing. No wavy air or sudden portal or a new storefront appearing out of thin air. She walked on, looking for signs, wondering if there would even be magical clues left behind.

Magic infused Earth now. And in a city like L.A. there were more than a few magical criminals prowling around looking for easy targets.

Even if it was annoying, Shay got it. The Gnome was keeping a low profile and had found a clever way to sort out intention before his shop became visible. *Smart.*

Hell, she wasn't a magical being, and she'd kept herself cloaked in the shadows of society. Though she would have never concealed herself inside a shopping mall. Just the right combination of brilliance and insanity.

Gah, weren't malls supposed to be dead a long time ago? Like some damned vampires.

A trio of college boys passed by her egging each other on with an elbow to the ribs and whispers. One turned his head back and let out a low whistle. She rolled her eyes and ignored them.

Yeah, keep dreaming.

Her mouth twitched as she navigated her way through the crowds, her heart thumping harder than normal. A tall Elf passed her, a small troll sitting on his shoulder. *Still not used to that.*

Her gaze continued to flick from person to person and store to store.

She wasn't worried about finding the Gnome. He might

have used magic to hide his shop, but she'd find it. The problem was everyone else.

Too many people meant too many targets to track. She'd killed more than a few people in the middle of malls and shopping centers in her old job. The marks never saw it coming. No one could keep track of everyone in the middle of a mall.

She wasn't meant to die in a kitchen, but in a mall. Shay shook her head, letting the thought go.

She continued to circulate around the second floor looking for the shop, grateful the mall only had two floors.

Wait, what was that? On her third loop, she saw it.

At first, her gaze slid across the entrance like it wasn't even there, but if she focused just off to the side, not looking at the opening directly she could make out the small gaming shop. There it was... a narrow door. A stylized cyan sign read, *Prophecy Gaming* and hung above the entrance.

Even after spotting it, Shay had trouble concentrating on perceiving the interior of the shop. Her eyes kept wanting to look everywhere but straight ahead.

Stop fucking with my mind.

Shay walked toward the door, keeping her focus off to the left. Her stomach felt like she was at the top of a roller coaster about to go over the edge. She stepped through the glamour and as her head cleared she could look straight ahead again. On either side of her were shelves to the ceiling filled with elaborate board and card games.

Why do you bother with all these if you make it so hard to find you to begin with? You could just be sitting in a room naked and no one would notice.

A short balding middle-aged man stood behind a counter, reading a book. *Game of Nations.*

Into thrillers... Odd choice for the proprietor of a gaming shop or a magic shop.

She eyed the man behind the counter and waited for him to look up from his book. He didn't stir as she loudly cleared her throat. The man looked up at her with total disinterest before returning his attention to his book.

"Good book?"

"Let's just say I can understand the power of obsession," the man replied, his gaze fixed on the book. "I can relate to George Clemente. Wallis might have had it coming."

"I'm here to see a Gnome."

"No Gnome works here. They can do better than minimum-wage retail. Anyone with the slightest bit of magic has better things to do."

Shay put both her hands on the counter and leaned forward. "No, he's here. Tubal-Cain. I *know* he's here." Peyton had given her the right name to use.

Still the man didn't blink. "You think a Gnome works in a random game shop in a mall?"

"This isn't a random game shop in a mall. It's protected by a glamour. I'm here aren't I? I want to see Tubal-Cain."

Tubal-Cain was the name of an ancient biblical blacksmith. She couldn't be certain he wasn't the same little dude mentioned in the Old Testament. A few spells would make it easy to convince bronze-age humans that you were one of them.

The man stared at her before setting his book down on the counter and closing it. "You don't want to buy a game. You're sure?"

"I want to buy something a lot more expensive than a game. Call him up, or cast a spell, or whatever you need to do because I'm not leaving until the Gnome shows up."

The man heaved a weary sigh. "And what would you need from a Gnome, anyway?"

"I have a job for him. I can pay and he's the guy I need."

"What sort of job?"

"Metal working."

"I see." The man nodded toward a door in the back of the shop. Shay followed behind him and he stopped at the door, stepping aside to motion to her to go in.

It was a small breakroom with two metal chairs around a plastic orange table. A wooden bookshelf stood in the corner of the room, filled with dogeared books. Shay scanned the titles but didn't see anything current. There was a row of Encyclopedia Brittanica taking up the entire bottom row. *Now, that is old.*

She turned around to ask the man a question but he was gone, replaced by a Gnome standing three feet tall and wearing a tidy dark suit and a fedora but no shoes on his large, bare feet.

The Gnome stared at her as his large, bulbous nose twitched. A red poppy on his bowler opened its petals and bared sharp little teeth, growling. "You've gone to a lot of trouble to find me, human."

"You're Tubal-Cain?"

"You can call me that... yes. And you are?"

"Shay."

"Why are you really here, Shay? Metal working? You don't need a Gnome for metal working."

"I need something special. A certain kind of knives. It's

not like I can get what I want from the Cutting Edge on the second floor."

"Knives? That's it? How boring."

Shay watched the Gnome, taking in every move. He was testing her, looking for her soft spots.

"Depends on the knives, don't you think... I'm interested in three knives. They need to be lightweight, never need to be sharpened and will never break." Shay counted each item on her fingers.

"Finding something like that depends on a lot of different factors. What do these knives need to cut?" Tubal-Cain tilted his head, staring at her with a scowl. The poppy let out a short, high-pitched howl.

"Throats mostly. Mostly humans, the occasional ice witch, a dragon somewhere in my future."

The Gnome gave a light chuckle. "Did a knife you own break in the throat of your enemy, lovely lady?"

"Something like that."

"And did this enemy deserve to die?"

Shay narrowed her gaze. *Another test.* "That's a philosophical question. I'd say yes, but a lot of people might disagree."

Tubal-Cain's scowl deepened, but he didn't say anything.

"Can you do it?"

"I can. But why should I? Why do I care if you have a sharp knife that never breaks?"

"You have a shop and I can pay. Seems pretty basic."

Tubal-Cain snorted. "With money? Your money isn't of interest to me. I have treasures you couldn't even begin to imagine. I'm not on Earth to earn dollars, that much I can guarantee."

Negotiation. Shay didn't have to be a master of magic or an expert on Oriceran psychology. *He likes the barter as much as the sale. Okay, let's go.*

Shay shrugged. "If you don't want money, what do you want? Everyone wants something."

"I should ask for your first-born child?" Tubal-Cain gave her a thin smile.

"Is this the part where if I guess your true name, you disappear in a huff after stamping your feet?"

The Gnome let out a cackle as the poppy hissed. "A feisty one, hmm?".

"Something like that." Shay smiled, resting her hand on the counter. "Look, you've parked yourself in a shrine to fast and easy sales on this planet. There has to be something I can get for you. I specialize in procuring things that are difficult to find. I can even retrieve items that are dangerous to find. We can work a trade if that's what it'll take."

Tubal-Cain moved over to one of the chairs and took a seat. It shrank to fit him comfortably.

"Know the myths of your own planet, human?"

"More than most people."

The Gnome lay one hand over another in his lap. "Adamantine."

"Like in Greek mythology?"

"Yes… *mythology*."

"Allegedly, a super-hard material. A lot of modern scholars claim that it's a just a general word that meant things like diamond and other hard materials and not an actual separate material."

Tubal-Cain nodded, a hint of disappointment in his features. "And what do you think?"

"I'm willing to take most ancient myths as a mixture of fiction and cold hard truth."

"Then you're more clever than many humans. That doesn't change the fact there are no natural sources of adamantine left on your planet." The Gnome grinned and rubbed his chin. "Bring me five pounds of adamantine metal. I'll make your knives out of it, and I'll keep the rest as my payment."

"That's it? You just want me to find some of this metal?"

"That's it." Tubal-Cain reached out to the center of the table. A small wooden box appeared.

Shay wasn't sure if he'd summoned it through a spell or if it'd always been there and hidden by magic.

"Take it," the Gnome said. "Three powerful knives. They'll serve you well enough for the moment, but their enchantment is limited." He opened the hinged lid to reveal three exquisite knives resting atop black velvet. "See?"

"You happened to have three knives sitting around?"

"There are a lot of things I have sitting around, Shay." The Gnome snapped the lid shut and pushed it toward her.

Shay picked the box up but kept her attention on the Gnome. "Why are you giving me something for nothing?"

"If you bring me the adamantine, it'd be more than worth your while." He gestured toward the box. "Their quality will show you what you could have for the rest of your limited life, but when the enchantment is gone, they will disappear, and you'll feel their loss, assuming you ever come back."

Shay scoffed. "Why wouldn't I come back?"

"I'm not convinced you can deliver me the adamantine." Tubal-Cain shrugged. "I don't care really either way, but on the small chance you can accomplish something useful, it's in my best interest to motivate you. Do well enough, I might even throw in a bonus."

"A bonus? Like what?"

"Something useful. That's all you need to know for now."

Shay lifted the case under her arm. "I'll get you your metal."

"We'll see." The poppy let out a cackle and closed its petals.

11

Shay settled in behind a computer set up on a table in Warehouse Five. Her fingers flew over the keyboard as she redirected her traffic behind yet another proxy server layer. Peyton had done well to point her at Tubal-Cain, and she appreciated his efforts, but the reminder of his usefulness also reminded her of something that continued to gnaw at her.

I can't let him have leverage over me.

There was no fucking way she was going to let anyone get away with having a dead man's switch that could reveal her existence to the world.

Now that she wasn't distracted by a tomb raiding job, and with the Gnome not in a hurry, she decided it was time to find out more about Peyton's little dead man's switch.

Its process was simple. Peyton had to check in at a server regularly or information about her would be sent out automatically. She suspected he was holding something back and there was more to it.

Just like I underestimated you, Peyton, you underestimated me. I know my way around a computer. I have more skills than I've been letting on and I plan to keep it that way. Not necessary to tell the world everything you know how to do.

Shay smiled at the thought.

It might have been easier to examine the computer he used at Warehouse Two, but she doubted she could get away with tampering with the computer without leaving a trail for him to follow. However, he was still working on a network she'd help set up. That gave her some advantage.

She'd been working on probing the dead man's switch for hours and she was closing in on the key links.

Shay pulled up the window containing network logs from around the date Peyton revealed he'd set up the failsafe. When she first started looking at the logs, she noticed there were no external logs listed after that timeframe. He must have anticipated what she would do, but never bothered to tell her.

Good for you, Peyton. Keep every advantage you have. Trust no one and verify. I'm an ex-killer for hire. I wouldn't trust me. Shit, I don't trust me.

Shay might have saved him from a hit, but he continued to impress her by demonstrating more savvy than she expected. That was the main reason she didn't put a bullet in his head when she found out he'd played her, even though she was sorely tempted.

Okay, I've got the general server connections, but there's something else here. Something else I'm missing. Just need to figure it out. She sat back, letting the information wash over her. *I can almost see it.*

"Peyton, you smart son of a bitch. How did you even think of this?"

She had made a fundamental assumption that all she needed to do was find the final server in the pathway and spoof the check-in signal, but the more she looked, the more holes she found.

The switch *wasn't* so simple. In fact, it was far from it.

Peyton had left out a few details in his overview of the switch. He'd set up real-world connections along his chain to thwart easy redirection of his network paths.

There were regular payments to several different accounts, along with regular third-party access to the server from different locations. She had found his proxies.

Shay didn't need to know who he was paying off, only the amounts so she could pay more and buy their silence.

"I didn't know you had it in you, but I'm still going to have to disable all this shit anyway. Sorry, Peyton."

Shay laced her fingers together and stretched her arms over her head. More than a little money needed to be spread around, and as backup she would have to redirect some of the final legs in the failsafe so she would know if anyone modified it, but soon Peyton wouldn't have any leverage over her.

Not that she planned to tell him. Never give away information.

Don't feel bad. You're smart, Peyton, but even with a dead man's switch, you're not paranoid enough.

Her watch beeped, and she glanced down. "Shit. I better get going."

Shay sipped on her coffee. "That doesn't sound like hiking, it sounds more like walking up and down stairs."

Bella laughed. "The stairs are part of the local experience. You're always saying how you want to see local stuff. It's urban hiking." Bella waved as Kara and Janelle stepped into the Silver Lake outpost of Alfred Coffee.

The two other women waved and headed into line to grab some coffee. Shay and Bella joined them.

"We all came ready to take it on in style." Their outfits helped. Their yoga pants, Lululemon for some, Patagonia for others, highlighted their toned legs.

Most wore single-shaded light tank tops, but Shay's shirt contained the outline of a glitter skull. An ironic call-out to her true nature.

It was also loose enough to allow her to conceal a knife in the small of her back. Much like the mall, jogging and hiking paths were great places to kill people. Shay knew from experience.

Huh. Where have I not killed someone? Don't think I've ever killed anyone in a church that I can remember. Wonder if that would win me points with Brownstone?

Once Kara and Janelle had their cups of coffee, the quartet pushed out of the coffee shop into the street.

Bella pointed across the street at a rising series of colorful stairs flanked by trees on one side. A single red heart covered several stairs near the bottom and the top. Various colors of paint decorated the stairs in-between.

"Those are the Micheltorena Stairs," Bella said. "I don't know if we're going to hit all six miles of stairs in the area. Most are decorated and they all have their own history and flair."

Kara took a sip of her coffee and looked back, pursing her lips, frowning.

"Something wrong with your coffee?" Shay pushed her foot against a stair, stretching her leg.

"I need something else..." Kara nodded toward a bar down the street. "Wait here. You want this? No? I'll be right back. I can't go hiking up and down that many stairs without something a little stronger to inspire." She poured the coffee on the ground as an old man clucked at her and jogged toward the bar.

The other three women laughed and waited for her to return. Soon she returned with her cup full of beer, the top firmly in place. "Much better. Let's go."

The women headed toward the Micheltorena Stairs that had the words, *in pursuit of magic* stenciled on them.

Guess we found it.

Shay felt herself relax. No tracking treasure over the internet, negotiating with ancient Oricerans, or gunning down cartel members. Just a simple hike around a neighborhood appreciating art with her friends.

Kara sipped her beer as they hit the bottom of the stairs. "I think I need to try harder to find a guy." She winced. "Sorry, Bella. I know you just broke up with your boyfriend."

"You did? You didn't mention it." Shay saw they were all distracted looking at Bella and took the opportunity to scan the steps. No one standing around in a suit trying to fit in. No one wearing a coat in the warm weather.

They continued making their way up the long flight of stairs, the colorful paint job making it more of an adventure. Some of the stairs were painted like piano keys, pointing out the song they were playing depending on where they stepped.

Bella gave a small smile. "I didn't want to bring everyone down. I looked up one day and realized I had a really good roommate. We realized we liked each other but don't love each other. It's getting easier and we're still on good terms."

Janelle was breathing harder, planting her entire foot as she stepped up. "That just leaves me with the only man right now. Not sure how that happened. Unless Shay's got something to tell us?"

I wonder how Brownstone would look in some tighter pants.

Shay's face warmed, and she prayed her friends would attribute it to the walk up the stairs, rather than her sudden embarrassment.

"Nope. Too busy to worry about men at the moment."

Damn it. Just because the guy has some muscles, can handle himself and isn't an idiot doesn't mean I should be thinking of him the first time someone mentions dating. I have other options. Kind of. Sort of.

"You better hold onto Darius. A good man is hard to find." *Picture anything but Brownstone.*

They all shared a laugh.

Just a normal, everyday life. No trouble. I could get used to this.

The group worked their way to another set of bright blue stairs and headed up, swinging their arms and keeping a good pace. Everyone was sweating and their breathing was labored except for Shay. She had a sheen as she breathed easily, taking in long breaths and holding back from sprinting up the stairs. She could feel the ache in her calves. *I should add stairs to the warehouse.*

Janelle brushed damp hair off her forehead and looked over at Shay. "Damn, Shay. You're not even breathing hard after three different sets of stairs. That's like a vertical mile. Are you running an obstacle course every night?"

Well, yeah, actually.

Shay laughed. "I jog a lot around the university."

Shay's watch let out a soft tweet. It was a Garmin Tactix Bravo GPS watch that she'd purchased after her recovery of the solid-gold owl in Paris. She looked down and saw there was a message from Peyton. A possible job. *Later.*

Bella looked at the watch and whistled. "Professors' salaries have gone up."

Shay forced a smile on her face. A sloppy mistake. The small details can expose lies.

"Boyfriend bling. A gift from an old boyfriend. He was trying to get back together with me by wallet slapping the honey."

"I thought you didn't have a man."

"I said he *tried*, not that he succeeded."

Her friends all laughed.

"What if he gives you a car?" Kara stopped on a stair, her hands on her knees.

"We'll just have to see." Shay winked and jogged ahead of her friends, checking the message from Peyton.

I'll explain the Fiat on the day they notice. Having normal friends was even better than meditation, taking her away from the darker parts of her life, but it did complicate things.

I'll need to be more careful next time.

No matter how close she grew to the women, they could never know the other side of her life. Shay's plan was to create two fully formed lives till they both were the truth.

Better plan next time. No big deal. At least none of these get togethers will end with me having to shoot anyone. I hope.

"Come on, girls," Shay shouted. "We still have seven more sets of stairs to see."

A mixture of laughs and groans arose from below her as she bounced in place, waiting patiently.

12

S hay relaxed in a Warehouse Two lounge chair reading the local paper on her iPad. She glanced over at the office where Peyton tapped away at his keyboard, a look of concentration on his face. He was researching the details of the new job.

He gave no sign that he knew his dead man's switch was disarmed.

Not so bad, if I do say so myself.

"I know you have a place all picked out. Think it over. This setup is looking pretty nice and I'm not sure you know the difference between a showdown online and a gun in your face. One will obliterate a lot of expensive equipment and the other flies through your brain pan. You listening?"

Peyton shot out of his chair and ran out of the office, planting himself in front of Shay.

Shay sat up with a frown. "What? I didn't know they still made madras suits."

"When did they ever stop? Focus."

"Hard to do with a human kaleidoscope in front of me. What'd you find?"

"Nice money. Great money. Like Smite-Williams-level money."

"I like hearing that. What's the job?"

Peyton lowered himself into the other lounge chair. "You know who Makar Kalinin is?"

Shay tilted her head as she tried to place the name. It seemed familiar, but the owner still escaped her. She gave up and shook her head.

"Russian oligarch, made his fortune in energy investment. He fell out of favor with the current government and had to high-tail it to Singapore a few years back. They claim he's a criminal scumbag. He claims *they* are criminal scumbags."

Shay nodded. "Oh yeah. I kind of remember him. Didn't someone try to assassinate his ass in the middle of the day while he was eating blinis?"

"Yeah. The guy has an army of security. The rumor is the guy's gotten very weepy and old-school about his Russian heritage now that's he's stuck in Singapore. Talked the restaurant into making his mother's recipe."

Shay snorted. "Yeah, I'm sure being a billionaire living in a mansion is a terrible life. Woe is him. How does he ever do it?"

"It does suck when you can't go where you want to go and live openly. Save it, I heard what you were saying. I'm still moving out." Peyton shrugged. "You have to let go some time."

"Always with the humor." Shay stared at him for a moment. "Fair enough. Go on."

"The short version of this is that Polish troops invaded Russia in the beginning of the seventeenth century. They basically grabbed anything that looked remotely valuable. They were supposed to have stuck the treasures on carriages bound toward Warsaw, but they didn't even reach Smolensk. The transports just kind of disappeared."

Shay shrugged, leaning over to finger the material on his jacket, frowning at him as he pulled away. "I'm focused. Some soldiers decided they could retire early. Not a big surprise. If I were some peon, I'd probably borrow a few gold coins from the local rich assholes myself."

"The thing is, there's nothing in the historical record to account for any unusual spike in wealth."

"It's not like every random thief leaves behind a detailed diary."

Peyton cleared his throat and smirked. "In this case, they kind of did, but not for the main treasure."

"Huh? Unpack that for me a little."

"It turns out a Russian force under a local nobleman was responsible for taking out the treasure train, and the nobleman leading that force was a distant ancestor of our potential client."

Shay squinted, folding her legs underneath. "But you said the treasure was lost."

"Well, yeah, it was lost. First by the Polish, and then by the Russians. But... it's not anymore. Not all of it, anyway."

"You're saying, what, we have directions?"

Peyton blew out a long breath and rubbed the back of

his neck. "Yeah, we do, but the directions are related to a map in a journal that was recently recovered. The journal was written by the nobleman leading the Russian force, but it's mostly about how they were being hunted."

"Hunted? By who? Polish troops?"

"Vodyanoy."

Shay furrowed her brow. It wasn't often she was completely clueless, but there was nothing to be gained by pretending otherwise.

"Who the hell is he?"

"Not a he, more of a *they*. River spirits who look like old men crossed with giant frogs. This ancestor of our client addressed the journal to his son. Basically, he talks about how they recovered the treasure, but they'd run afoul of some vodyanoy who wanted the treasure as a tribute."

"It could be bullshit. Some guy just making an excuse to explain why the treasure disappeared."

"Do you really believe that?"

Shay shook her head. "I wish I could. I'll bet the Russians didn't give up the treasure?"

"Not at first, and what followed was your standard monster horror movie plot until only the guy writing the journal was left with one other person. He'd tried to appease the vodyanoy by finally giving up the treasure, but by then it wasn't enough." Peyton shivered, pulling his jacket closer. "The creatures wanted something else."

"What the fuck did they want?"

"A gold locket the man was wearing. It had a single dried iris petal inside. It was a gift from the man's wife. He decided that he'd be betraying her if he gave it up to some random river monsters."

Shay blinked hard a few times. "So, wait. Let me get this straight. This guy was dropping treasure all over the place like he didn't care after *everyone* was killed, but he wouldn't give up a locket with a flower? I don't know if I should be impressed or find some spell that sends me back in time so I can slap the man upside the head for being a fucking moron."

Peyton relaxed back into the chair. "In the end, he knew the vodyanoy were closing in, so he found an abandoned church and hid in the basement. He thought even if the place wasn't in use, the vodyanoy wouldn't follow him onto consecrated ground. From what his journal says, he was right, but they also wouldn't leave. They always had someone there, guarding the area, like they were obsessed with getting that locket."

"So, what he died in a church basement, waiting out some water monsters?"

"Yes and no. Like I said, there was one surviving person with him, some servant kid. The man thought the monsters hadn't killed him because he was a virgin and not as tainted."

"Interesting theory."

"They had a decent amount of food left because everyone else in their group had already died, so they spent a couple of months digging tunnels from the basement, and then the nobleman gave the journal to the kid, along with a sack of coins and told him to get the hell out of there while he distracted the monsters."

"Sacrificing the kid?"

Peyton shook his head. "Nope, there is some writing after the last entry of the nobleman, different handwriting.

It relates how the kid made it to a nearby village. The nobleman made a big show, including his locket, to keep the monsters away from the kid. He mostly just wanted the kid to escape and get the story out there to his family."

"But the journal got lost," Shay pointed out.

"Lost until recently."

Shay processed the entire bizarre story and shook her head. "Wait a second. He gave up all the original treasure."

"Yeah, he did. And there's no indication that it's still in the area."

"Then what the fuck does this Kalinin guy want me to find?"

Peyton tapped his chest. "The *locket*. That man was his direct ancestor, and he's really into the idea that the locket represents the spirit of defiance of his family even under the harshest of conditions. it has something to do with him being in exile."

Shay stared at Peyton. It wasn't that she didn't believe the story. Weirder shit had already happened, but it was hard to believe anyone would care that much about an otherwise useless artifact. Sentiment was as foreign to her as Light Elf language.

"And this locket is magical?" She let her doubt color her voice.

"No, not according to legend or the client. But he's willing to pay three million for its recovery, and he's willing to send us a copy of the map from the journal that he believes leads to it. So other than doing background research to double-check, most of the hard prep work's already over."

Shay pushed out of her chair with a frown. "Something's fishy about that."

Peyton laughed, but stopped when faced with her glare. "Wait. You weren't making a joke about the vodyanoy?"

"No." Shay ran a hand through her hair. "If he has a map, and it's just some stupid locket with dried-up flower dust, why does he need a tomb raider? Even if he's in exile, he could hire a kid to do it. Nice symmetry with the legend."

"Yeah. That's the tricky part. You'd be the fourth person he hired."

"What?"

"Every other person he's hired has been found floating dead in a river near the church ruins," Peyton said.

"Yeah, that would explain the money. And no one finds this suspicious?"

Peyton shrugged. "Local authorities said they all looked like suicides. Kalinin has upped the price every time and gotten more selective about who he's hiring. This time he's looking for a *top-tier* tomb raider."

Shay took a deep breath. "Okay, let's assume some angry frogmen are guarding this locket." Her gaze drifted to her holster. "Legend say these frog assholes are bulletproof?"

"The journals say the Russians managed to take one down with musket fire, and his friends dragged him off."

"My Glock is a lot more impressive than some old-school musket." Shay grinned. "I think I'm about to make an easy three million."

Shay checked the GPS on her phone as she pulled the Burlak SUV off the road. The ruins of the church lay close to a small village only a couple of hours away from Moscow. She didn't know if she was chasing bullshit or not, but the client coughed up a hundred thousand dollar deposit once he learned Shay's cover name, Aletheia the field archaeologist would look into it.

Her false online identity served her well in protecting her, even if some, like the Professor, had seen through it. She wasn't willing to burn it, given how she'd already built up a nice reputation focused around the name.

My reputation is starting to mean something. I like that. Eventually I won't even need to hide so much.

Her vehicle shook as the terrain grew rougher. She slowed at the increased tree density. The ruins were only minutes away.

The plan was simple. She'd follow the map to the church, find the locket, and then haul ass back to Moscow to hop a supersonic back to America. If any frogmen dared showed their ugly-ass faces, she'd let them experience the joys of modern Austrian-made firearms.

It is kind of weird that they haven't done anything about these ruins. There were some decent-sized towns nearby, and the local village is practically on top of this place. Then again, all that treasure is still in Lake Toplitz and people already had a good idea it was there.

The vodyanoy might be preventing the villagers from doing much, but that was nothing a few Russian soldiers with rifles couldn't accomplish.

Shay slammed the brakes and yanked her pistol out, her

heart pounding. Several seconds passed before she realized the bulbous-eyed frogman in front of her wasn't an actual vodyanoy but a statue.

Damn it.

Thirteen stone statues formed a perimeter around the collapsed and mostly plant-covered ruins of the church. If she didn't have directions and GPS, she could see how she might have trouble finding the place.

Shay narrowed her eyes. The gray statues lacked any plants on them or any signs of weathering. It was as if they were carved yesterday.

Fuck. For all I know, they were. Creepy. The locals wanted to scare kids away from messing with the church grounds. Or this is their way of trying to honor the frog boys and keep their ass away from the village.

Her stomach knotted, and she swept her gaze back and forth. No hostiles. At least none that she could see.

Shay got out of her car. The statues weren't doing anything, and no actual frog monsters showed up. She pulled a loaded tactical harness, backpack, and her AR goggles out of the back.

"At least this shit isn't under water," she muttered.

She crept toward the ruins, her gun out. The statues continued to be unimpressive if ugly, but a sensation of being watched lingered as the hair on the back of her neck stood on end and her shoulders tightened. Something's not right.

It's 400 years later. I let that weird story get in my head. Just because a lot of magical shit in the past turned out to be true doesn't mean it all is.

Vodyanoy might not be watching her, but there were plenty of other dangerous beings who might be, including the most unpredictable of all, greedy humans.

Just in and out. I can do this. Fuck Russian frogmen. I've faced a Russian Ice Witch.

13

Shay approached the tangle of overgrown plants, rotted wood, and stone that marked the ruins of the church. Every few steps, she surveyed the area again to see if she could catch sight of whoever must be out there making her feel like she was being watched.

No one bothered to shoot at her. They didn't want an easy kill or they didn't care about only her presence in the area.

Could be someone else is trying to grab the locket and using me to do the hard part. Doesn't matter, asshole. I know you're there.

Shay's gaze swept the area as she stepped into the ruins. No traps. No bodies, frogman or human. No scoring or burns on the walls. Nothing to suggest a battle occurred at the church recently.

The journal said the creatures couldn't get closer to the church, and it was already abandoned. It makes sense there was no epic battle, and it's not like the guy had cannons with him.

The suicides of the previous recovery teams weighed

heavy on Shay's mind even if she knew she had better killing skills. She wasn't immune to magic, and she needed to make sure no one disabled her with a spell.

All she needed was one good shot.

I should have brought some grenades after all.

Her follow-up research on the vodyanoy didn't show much in the way of mind-control abilities, but they were associated with unexplained drownings. The general strategy involved dragging people under the water and holding them there.

I'll just stay away from the river. No frogmen can drag my ass under.

Shay reached the back of the ruins and found a worn staircase leading into darkness. She slipped her AR goggles on and activated the infrared mode. There were no unusual thermal traces down the stairs or around the area other than a few nearby birds. If someone were hiding and watching her, they knew well enough to keep out of sight.

A fetid smell assaulted Shay's nose as she made her way down the stairs and to the doorway where the rotted remnants of a wooden table lay on the ground. She switched her goggles to normal mode and pulled out a flashlight.

The expansive and cool stone basement floor was mostly empty except for torn and moldy paper fragments littering the ground. Moss and vines covered the room. Shay gasped as she realized the room had once held books that the centuries had long since taken back. The bits and pieces were all that remained.

What a fucking waste.

To Shay's surprise, a few wooden crates remained

intact in the corner. She used her boot to nudge open a box. Vestments lay inside, their colors muted by time and riddled with holes from centuries of providing food to insects.

An irregular large opening in the wall led deeper underground.

Must be what he and the kid dug out.

Tension suffused Shay's body. Even though she'd lost the sensation of being watched, other instincts pushed relaxation away.

Too easy. If anyone could just walk in and grab this thing, Kalinin would have never gotten around to hiring me. There's some trick somewhere, and I'm not seeing it coming. But why?

Shay lacked any decent info on whether any of the previous teams made it to the actual church, but at least their deaths didn't support the idea of the church and the tunnels being filled with traps.

The shadows emitted a shuddering noise as Shay whipped out her gun. Several rats rushed toward the other side of the room, their nails scratching along the ground and their squeaks echoing in the chamber.

Shay made a sweep of the room with her gun outstretched, confirming no one was hiding their movement underneath the blanket sound of the rats' movement. The rats weren't a problem unless they were magical Oriceran rats. Otherwise she didn't give a shit. Still, she kept her gun out.

The tunnel broke off into two smaller tunnels and Shay had to crouch to make it through them. Debris and half-decayed litter lay about, but her thermal checks didn't suggest anything unusual other than a few bones that looked suspiciously human. Everything about the tunnel was as expected after being unused for centuries.

Shay stopped and pointed her flashlight at the ground. Footprints. Boots from the look of it, not fresh but not from the seventeenth century either.

"Someone was here. A wild goose chase? Good thing there's a hundred k deposit."

The tunnel curved and led to a larger dug-out chamber. A skeleton lay against the wall, its arms crossed over its chest. The lack of clothing or any hint of flesh suggested it had been there for enough time to have been licked clean. All that remained was a golden locket that hung around its neck.

She checked the ground. The boot prints went all the way up to the skeleton. They could have recovered the necklace.

What the fuck happened? Boot prints from villagers instead of tomb raiders?

"The frogmen never got what they wanted. Good for you, pal. Way to show those assholes until the end of time."

Shay looked down at the skeleton. A shining example of determination mixed with suicidal stubbornness.

For the first time on a job, real guilt stabbed at her.

"Sorry, pal. But at least this is going to your ancestor and not some random thief."

Shay paused to use her AR goggles to check the skeleton through several frequency ranges. It wouldn't help her detect any magical traps, but it was better than nothing.

Satisfied she was as prepared as she was going to be, she reached out and gently lifted the locket over the skull.

The ground didn't shake. She heard no distant explosions or water rushing into the tunnels. No sudden screeches or the sound of spears flying at her head.

Shay sucked in a breath. Her heart pounded at the lack of an obvious trap. She refused to believe the job would be so straight-forward. She had to be missing something.

A curse. That was one possibility. She had not run into a true curse yet, but it'd come eventually. That only made it more important for her to build connections with the magical world. Preventive medicine.

Shay gently opened the locket. There was no iris petal inside anymore, only a fine white dust. Even the most stubborn man's effort couldn't defeat time.

"Three million for pride and loyalty, huh?"

She shook her head. Kalinin was an exile from his home with hostile people trying to kill him. He was a lot like her in that sense, but he wasn't running away and erasing his past. Instead, he was still pushing back, as if he could wait out his enemies and come back to reclaim his place in society.

"This is not what I want. It's not like my old life was solid enough to build on anything lasting."

The attempt on her life provided a convenient excuse, but Shay couldn't deny that she'd grown sick of being a hitman long before Natalie showed up to die in her kitchen.

Three million would help her find a new life or reclaim an old one if wanted.

Shay wrapped the locket in a soft felt cloth, slipped it into a small tan leather bag, and stowed it in her backpack before making her way back around the tunnels, her gun at the ready. Even if there were no traps, that didn't mean there was no ambush.

The trip back to the basement was uneventful, the silence oppressive from the lack of danger. By the time Shay emerged back into the surface ruins, she began to wonder if she was just damned lucky.

If Kalinin hired a few amateurs, they might have just got picked off by some local thugs or something.

Not a big deal after all.

Shay laughed quietly. Sometimes you get paid well just to be brave. She crept along further, her gun raised but the sensation of being watched returned and all her senses went on alert. She spun, seeking any sign or hint of someone else. The grass, trees, and shrubs still looked empty of any real threats.

"Wait a second," Shay whispered. She pointed her gun at a vodyanoy statue and counted. "One." The Glock jumped to another statue. "Two... three... four... five... six..." She winced and felt a chill go down her spine. "Oh shit."

Thirteen. She was sure there were thirteen before, but now there were only six. Either the world's most efficient vandals had shown up during her brief time underground, or seven frogmen were now on the move.

Shay flipped her AR goggles down and again did a thermal sweep. Nothing large or humanoid stood out.

Fuck. Would this even work, or is a frogman the temperature of the surrounding air? I mean he's a magical frogman... damn it. It hurts my brain to think about it.

Shay flipped the goggles back up and jogged toward the

SUV. She needed to get the hell out of there before she ended up face down in the river.

Something crunched behind her. Shay spun and fired on reflex.

A high-pitched squeal filled the air.

"What... the... fuck?"

Her victim fell to the ground, green blood spewing from the wound in its head. Frogman from hell was an accurate description, and Shay's heart rate picked up at seeing the monster in the flesh rather than in statue form.

It had two legs with webbed feet and two arms ending in long claws. Its bulbous eyes dominated its face along with a maw filled with razor-sharp teeth. A layer of a thick liquid covered its body. It was slime or mucous, Shay wasn't sure.

The color of the air near the vodyanoy was wrong, and the shadows were not right. The air shimmered as six more frogmen appeared.

Shay emptied her clip, putting two rounds into each of the remaining monsters. Several quick, ragged breaths followed as she reloaded her gun.

Shay sprinted for her vehicle, not wanting to wait around for reinforcements. She threw open the door and slid into the seat, starting the SUV even as her foot was on the gas pedal. An odd choking and thumping sounded as the engine turned over, but the vehicle started up.

"What the fuck?"

The dashboard displays were all in Russian, but the icons were understandable enough. Somehow she'd gone from a full tank of gas to being almost empty, her oil pressure was shit, and her engine was in dire need of immediate service. Several other problems afflicted the vehicle, but she couldn't interpret the language or the symbols.

Shay revved the engine and pulled away. She might not be able to get back to Moscow with the SUV, but she could at least get to the nearby village and put enough space between her and the lizard kingdom.

There she could rent a vehicle from a villager. The fact that the village could exist in the area for centuries without much trouble told her the vodyanoy weren't willing to go near a concentration of people.

Not like those fuckers were bullet proof.

Shay glanced into her rearview mirror, and bile rose in her throat.

The vodyanoy corpses were all gone. "Let's hope that means they disappear when they die."

Shay smacked the steering wheel. "Stay with me, you stupid piece of shit. Stay with me."

14

Peyton stifled a yawn and glanced down at the time on the computer. Dawn was coming soon in L.A., but it was still afternoon near Shay's tomb raid site. She had not sent him a message since arrival, but that wasn't unusual.

His computer beeped, and Peyton frowned. He clicked on a notification window and read the alerts. They were automated messages attached to monitoring programs he'd set up and focused on Shay's Aletheia identity. Someone was poking around.

Peyton read through the messages. A few forum questions here and there, a few network tracing operations elsewhere. It was another tomb raider, Johann Weiss, who had taken an extreme interest in discovering the real person behind Aletheia.

They still had a long way to go before they connected Aletheia with any of the warehouses or Shay, but they held enough puzzles pieces that Peyton's stomach churned a little.

"Time to tell Shay."

Peyton lifted his phone. His finger hovered over her coded name in his contact list: ASB queen. Ass-kicking snark bitch queen. It was too hard to fit pizza lover in there.

No. Shay was on a job and needed to concentrate, especially since it seemed like a milk run. Peyton might not be a former killer or current tomb raider, but he knew that something that looked too easy from the outside always had hidden complications.

He was the tech specialist, and he was the one who'd set up most of her current identity online. It was time to take some initiative and send the bastard on a wild goose chase.

Peyton cracked his knuckles. "Okay, tomb boy, time to show you my skills."

This is dumb. Shay would wave her gun at me if she knew what I was doing.

Backpack over his shoulder, Peyton stepped off the escalator and took a right, which brought him to the baggage claim and rental car areas of Dane County Regional Airport. Hardly the place a person would expect to find an exotic tomb raider.

Few people were in the small airport that late morning.

Of all the places Peyton ever imagined himself visiting, Madison, Wisconsin, wasn't high on the list. He took the fastest route possible and booked a supersonic flight to Chicago, driving up to Madison in a rental car.

He'd laid down enough electronic bread crumbs to convince Johann that Shay was interested in a fictional ancient Native American artifact buried under a Walmart in Madison. The plan wasn't the greatest, but Peyton was fortunate that he'd traced Johann's latest activity to Michigan. There was no way the man would be able to resist.

The electronic trail was enough. I didn't have to come out here just to confirm his actual arrival. Since when do I do field work?

Peyton lacked any checked luggage and headed over to the rental car window to pick up the Hyundai Elantra he'd booked under a fake name.

Freedom.

The whole point of him taking a little jaunt to the Upper Midwest was to prove to Shay he wasn't some chair drone who couldn't get his hands dirty and to be of service to Shay. It helped that Johann wasn't a hitman. He had no reason to be looking for someone like Peyton.

Even if she found out what he'd done, in the end, she would understand. *She might be a bitch at times, but she can see the value in taking a risk to get something done.*

A short exchange later, Peyton was driving away from the airport in a blue Elantra, whistling to himself and driving toward the Walmart.

He'd seeded specific times for Shay's arrival and tomb raid, along with some tantalizing fake information that would have Johann convinced she was a Japanese woman. Peyton only wanted to get eyes on Johann to confirm the deception worked.

Once that was accomplished, he could leave and

continue laying out similar false paths elsewhere for the rival tomb raider.

"This is easy. Not going to kill anyone. Not going to dig up some ancient dragon's gold. Just going to look around for some German guy, and then I'll go home. Easy as pie, and I'll þe back before Shay knows what's up." He just about had himself convinced.

Peyton looked down at his phone. Shay's only contact with him in the last several hours was a brief text.

Car trouble. Will contact you again when I get to Moscow.

He'd made sure to bring his computer, so he could back her up if she needed quick hacking or research help, but he didn't bother to inform her that he'd left not only the warehouse but the state.

She'll probably pull a gun on me again when she gets back. But, if she didn't kill me over the dead man's switch, she's not going to kill me over helping her out.

Dane County was a poor rival for Los Angeles County in size and population, and a quick half-hour brought him to the Walmart. He parked across the street in a bank's parking lot and fished binoculars out of his backpack.

It was almost time for Shay's alleged arrival at the Walmart. If Johann was any good, he would likely already be in position at the store.

Peyton searched from vehicle to vehicle for any sign of the rival tomb raider. No one matching the man's description sat in the parking lot or emerged from the store.

He lowered his binoculars when something flashed in his rearview mirror. He looked up and his heart skipped a beat.

Johann Weiss sat in an Audi right behind him.

Okay, it worked. Be cool. He just had the same idea I did about surveillance. Time to get going.

Peyton swallowed and started the car. He slowly pulled out of the parking lot and looked in his rearview mirror. Johann was following him.

"Oh shit."

The fake IDs Peyton prepared for the trip would stand up to an easy inspection, but not anything deep. He was not up for attracting the attention of the police. That meant a screaming car chase through downtown Madison was probably a bad idea.

"Okay, it might be a coincidence."

Peyton turned down a side street at random. The Audi remained behind him.

"I should have brought a gun. A big gun. Or a long, pointy knife."

He left town too fast to make arrangements to smuggle a gun aboard or even openly pack one in a checked baggage. He was only supposed to be doing some surveillance and didn't worry about being able to defend himself.

Peyton sped up, not pushing much past the speed limit. The Audi matched his speed. More abrupt turns didn't dislodge the car from right behind him. He wasn't even trying to be subtle.

"Wait. I'm thinking about this the wrong way." Peyton pulled into a parking lot of a McDonald's and drummed his fingers on his steering wheel as the Audi parked a few spots down from him.

Johann Weiss wasn't going to gun him down in the

middle of the day in public. Peyton needed to do what Shay would do. Confront the man with style.

He glanced around to confirm the people inside the restaurant and some on the street had a good line of sight. Witnesses meant protection.

Peyton told himself that a few times before exiting the car and marching over toward Johann with all the swagger he could muster, digging his shaking hands into the pockets of his electric green pants.

The muscular, heavyset German tomb raider stepped out of his vehicle and walked around to the passenger's side. He leaned against the car, his thick arms crossed over his chest.

"Why you following me, man?" Peyton said.

"Who said I'm following you?" Johann pressed his lips together in a thin smile.

Time for a little bluster.

"I know you're following me and I should call the cops. Let them run your name and see if there are a bunch of warrants out on you."

Johann leaned forward and lowered his voice. "I think you'll find that any crimes I've ever committed are unknown to the authorities."

"Whatever. You don't know who you're fucking with." Peyton squared his shoulders, but the other man loomed over him and could probably bench press him with a single arm. He wasn't sure how much the attempt at intimidation registered.

Johann gave him a feral smile. "You're right about one thing, *hosenscheisser.* I don't know who you are and I don't care. I only care about one thing. The Goddess of Truth is mine."

Johann looked Peyton up and down and snorted. "Who are you? Some college boy who decided he'd make quick money pretending to be a tomb raider? I'll give you credit for being able to follow the Japanese bitch's trail."

Peyton frowned, but he could work with Johann's mistakes. If Johann thought Peyton was another inexperienced rival, that worked out far better than if he found out Peyton was a friend of the target. Peyton's fake information was proving to be convincing enough.

"You know what the problem is with a lot of people?" Peyton asked.

"What?"

"They forget that you don't need big muscles to do magic." Peyton's best impression of a dark Shay grin followed.

Johann's face twitched. "Don't threaten me, *hosenscheisser.*"

"You going to kill me in the middle of a McDonald's parking lot?"

Johann's right hand lifted the inside of his jacket.

Oh shit. He is going to kill me in the middle of a McDonald's parking lot. I did not see that coming.

Peyton saw his one chance and leaped forward, shoving his bony knee into the man's crotch. Johann let out a loud groan and crumpled to the ground.

Oh shit. Oh shit. Oh shit.

Peyton yanked the back off his watch and pulled out a small silver disc. He threw it at the Audi. It exploded in sparks on contact. It was enough to fry at least some of the electronics in the vehicle and slow down the tomb raider.

He ran for the Elantra, throwing open the door and started the car before the door was even shut.

Johann pushed himself off the ground but didn't go for a gun or charge at Peyton.

"Nice lucky hit, but you'll be dead by tomorrow, *hosenscheisser*." He stood in the middle of the parking lot, yelling.

Peyton peeled away from the McDonald's toward the highway.

He'd done it. He'd confirmed he could mislead someone like Johann Weiss. And now he also had a man who wanted him dead. Well, another anyway.

Is this how Shay feels after every job?

Peyton drove for 20 minutes. He'd checked the mirrors several times, but there was no sign of the tomb raider or his Audi. The EMP disc must have worked.

"Need to get out of this state, ASAP."

Peyton yanked out his phone and booked a seat on a flight under yet another false name he maintained with just enough of a trail to comfort the TSA. The flight wasn't supersonic, but it left in less than an hour, and he was only twenty minutes away from the airport. Soon, he'd be back on his way to L.A., and the only thing Johann would be was frustrated with the lack of any Native American artifacts underneath the local Walmart.

Yeah. I'm better at this than I thought.

Peyton rubbed his hands together as he waited for the gate attendant to announce boarding. He'd not bothered to check in the Elantra. He was burning the fake identity anyway, and they would eventually find it in the airport parking lot.

Need to get the hell out of here.

Johann likely returned to the Walmart to try and intercept his original target. There was no reason for him to put in a lot of effort hunting Peyton down. At least, Peyton hadn't spotted the man anywhere, and it wasn't like Captain Super-German would have been hard to spot.

A black-haired woman swayed toward where Peyton was seated. Her eyes were bloodshot and half closed.

The woman stumbled at the last moment, falling forward. Peyton reached out to hold her off of him as something sliced his hand and he winced.

"I'm so sorry." The woman's speech was slurred. She pushed away from Peyton, looking past him. "Oh, I'm not even at the right gate." She giggled. "Sorry again." The woman spun on her heel and walked away, swaying the whole time.

One of her long, blue nails was covered in blood. Peyton glanced down at his hand. She must have cut him when she fell.

Well, if the worse that I got was a little nail cut from all of this, I'm doing pretty well. Wonder how Shay's doing?

15

The Burlak was a total loss from what Shay could get out of the mechanic's broken English. Her Russian was all but non-existent, and the conversation wasn't all that enlightening until the man showed her the shredded lines below the vehicle and the damage under the hood.

To the mechanic's credit, he didn't seem to question why there were so many obvious claw marks on and inside her vehicle.

There were no car rental places in the village, and no locals were willing to turn over their car for a little while in exchange for cash. That left her the only choice of a bus that left once a day in the morning, and she'd already missed it.

I should just fucking walk back to Moscow.

Instead, Shay headed for the only café in town and took a seat at the counter. She chowed down on a grilled ham and cheese sandwich. No one paid her much attention, but she also didn't know if they were talking about her at all.

A beautiful redhead stepped into the café as the other patrons and the owner looked her way and tensed.

What do we have here? Local queen bee?

The woman was several years younger than Shay with a pale complexion and slender build. Elaborate floral patterns covered her maxi dress. She glided over toward Shay and sat next to her without a word.

"Can I help you?" Shay kept both her hands above the table in case she needed to go for a weapon.

"No, but I can help you. I'm Irina." Her accent was Russian but with an odd inflection.

"Unless you have a car you can give me, you can't help me."

"Oh, but I do have a car I can give you, and I'm aware of your trouble with your rental vehicle."

Shay raised an eyebrow and took another bite of her sandwich, letting the time tick by. "In some postage-stamp-sized town like this, I can't be surprised that everyone knows my business. Why do you want to help me?"

"Because it'll annoy certain people I don't like."

Shay laughed. "What? Your townies don't appreciate a tourist?"

"Something like that. I find them backward and short-sighted." Irina sighed and shook her head. "The world has moved on, but they still cling to old traditions."

"Look, I can pay if you have a car I can rent."

"You don't need to pay. Not with money."

Shay narrowed her eyes. "You can't want to fuck with these people that much."

"We all have those that annoy us." The woman folded her hands in front of her on the counter.

Shay dipped her gaze for a moment. The woman's dress remained dry, but water leaked from her hands, and a small pool was forming on the table. Further inspection of her legs and feet showed water under her as well. The woman was like a leaky faucet.

Shay considered going for her weapon, but if she gunned down a woman in the middle of a café, everyone in town could descend on her. It was too close to call.

She could take them, but massacring an entire village seemed excessive, even for her.

Killing a woman for being wet probably wouldn't work as a justification.

"What the fuck are you?" Shay muttered. "You the Queen of the Frogmen or something?"

Irina scowled. "Don't ever compare me to those disgusting vodyanoy. This country would be better off without their kind, even if they do have their uses on occasion."

"Okay, sorry. If it makes you feel any better, I took out a batch near the old church ruins."

At least I think I did.

The watery woman responded with a scoff. "You shot them?"

"Yeah. They went down. They bled."

Then they disappeared.

Irina sighed. "They've already healed. They can't come into the village because they fear me, but if you leave in my vehicle, they can't hunt you. And they'll return in far greater numbers than you faced before."

Fucking wonderful. I didn't actually kill any of them.

Shay shook her head. "I still don't understand who you are."

"Some might refer me to me as a *rusalka*. Some would say I'm an evil spirit. Some would say I'm a ghost, but the truth is, I'm a woman who carries an ancient grudge. I was wronged in an old life, and I was given a chance at another. This village is mine and I intend to improve it."

"Okay, so how do I fit into all of this?"

"You came to recover that wretched locket, I presume, and you have it. The vodyanoy wouldn't be after you otherwise."

Shay wondered if she should lie but decided against it. Pissing off some strange Russian water spirit wasn't high on her list of survivable encounters. "The frogmen killed the rest of the people who have gone after it?"

"I've lost count over the last couple of centuries how many fools have come for it. The vodyanoy take them to the river as sacrifices to me." Irina laughed softly. "It's a quaint gesture and unnecessary anymore. I've found better ways to gain my power."

"But you want to help me escape?"

"Yes."

"Why?"

Irina's eyes gleamed with curiosity. "Because you're the first woman to come for the locket, and there's something I sense in you. A destiny, perhaps. Something great or something horrible, but still grandiose. I want to see where that goes, and I don't think it ends with you being drowned in our local river."

Shay blinked. "I don't have a special destiny. I'm just a tomb raider."

Sure, I used to be a hitman, but it's not like those are rare in this world.

"And I just used to be nothing more than a farmer's daughter." The woman put out her palm. A single key lay there in a pool of water.

Shay pushed her plate away. "There's something else. Something you're not telling me."

Irina tilted her head. "Does it matter as long as you get what you want?"

"It does not." *Is this the part where I lose my soul?*

"Go now," Irina said. "Take the locket. They'll wander away from the area once it's gone." The rusalka nodded to a blue Marussia sitting outside. The sports car was wildly out of place in the modest and small village.

Shay snatched up the key. No one got something for nothing. Irina was using Shay to get rid of the frogmen.

Works for me.

Shay didn't plan to return to this village ever. She didn't care if she was changing some sort of local balance of supernatural power. All she cared about was doing her job and getting paid. She doubted that some rusalka could take over Russia single-handedly.

"Thanks for the assist."

Irina smiled, brushing her hair off her shoulder. "You're welcome. Someday come back and visit."

"I'm gonna have to go with a hard no for that request."

The trip back to Moscow proceeded without any strange encounters, supernatural or otherwise. Once Shay checked in for her flight and made it past security, she called Peyton to check in.

After several rings, the call went to voice mail.

"Huh. He must be in the bathroom."

Shay sent him a text.

Found the perfect jewelry. Made a new friend. Won't be bringing her with me. Tell you about it when I get back. Boarding my flight soon.

Shay yawned as she stepped off the jetway into the boarding area. Exhaustion had seeped into every cell in her body, but it was still early evening L.A. time, which meant her helpful hacker would still be awake.

Peyton had never responded to her text, which was unlike him. But he could be obsessing over a programming task and forgot about the outside world.

Or out apartment hunting while I'm away.

Shay tried calling him. Again, it went to voice mail. She frowned, the slightest prick of concern settling into her chest.

Why the fuck aren't you answering? I'm not your girlfriend. I'm the woman who holds your life in her hands.

She checked the security systems on all the warehouses from her phone. Everything was all green.

Shay started looking at the feed from each Warehouse Two camera. She spotted Peyton underneath the covers in his bed.

Taking a nap this early? He must have stayed awake all night to support me. Doesn't mean I won't bust his balls about it.

"Time to go check in."

"Hey, Peyton," Shay yelled as she entered the cubicle maze.

Even if he was asleep, he almost always woke up when she drove into the warehouse. It was hard to sleep through a massive metal door opening and closing and a sports car driving in.

Shay arrived at the man's bedside.

Peyton lay there, his sheets and clothes sweat-soaked. He'd not even changed into pajamas. Vomit stained the bed and the floor, and the man looked as a green as a vodyanoy.

His eyes fluttered open. "Shay..." he moaned. "I made a big mistake."

Shay blinked. "I hope you didn't eat that chicken I told you to throw out."

"Assassin... poisoned me. I think."

Shay forced down every retort or angry question that wanted to bubble up. Instead, she needed to confirm one thing before she could focus on him.

"Has the warehouse been compromised?"

Peyton managed to shake his head. "No. Got me... outside of the warehouse. Way far away."

"Fuck." Shay hurried over to the bed and lifted the sick researcher, draping his arm over her shoulder. "We need to get you some help. I reserve the right to kill you myself some day."

"Hospital?"

"Fuck no. They get their hands on your DNA, it'll raise questions we don't want to answer. It's time for you to meet Dr. Chao."

"He'll live," said Dr. Chao, almost sounding disappointed. The balding Chinese-American man moved over to a sink to wash his hands after disposing of his thin blue gloves. "I've managed to neutralize the poison, but you're lucky you brought him in when you did. Fast-acting shit. Nasty."

"Can I talk to him?"

The doctor shrugged. "Sure. He's awake, if weak. Don't have him do anything strenuous for a while."

Shay chuckled. "Normally, he doesn't." She pulled out her phone and brought up a custom app, giving it a few taps. "Your payment is on the way."

"He can stay the night if you need, but for now, I'm going to sleep." Dr. Chao gave her a tired smile and pushed through the door linking his make-shift clinic room to a hallway in the rest of his house.

Shay went and sat on the edge of Peyton's bed. "Spill it. How the fuck did you end up on death's door when you should have just been chilling in the warehouse?"

"I did something that paid off till it didn't."

"Be more specific."

Peyton let out a groan quickly followed by a gassy belch. "I found out another tomb raider was close to tracking you down through your online identity. I messed with him, put him off the track."

"When did it stop paying off?"

"Part of it involved me confirming directly that they'd taken the bait."

Shay narrowed her eyes. "And what does confirming directly mean, exactly?"

"It means I flew to Madison to gets eyes on the mark. A rival tomb raider, Johann Weiss."

"Are you fucking kidding me? Johann Weiss isn't a guy you wanted to fuck with. He's not as ruthless as me, but he's damned close." Shay groaned and rubbed a hand over her face. "That was stupid. So, what, Weiss spotted you and poisoned you?"

"Nope. I kneed him in the balls when I confronted him." Peyton belched again. "EMPed his car so he couldn't follow me and headed straight back to the airport. *He* didn't come after me."

Shay arched a brow. She didn't know Peyton had it in him. "Nice moves."

"Yeah, but he had someone at the airport, a chick faking being drunk. She scratched me with one of her nails. I didn't think anything about it until I got back and started throwing up. By the time I knew I needed help, I could barely think." Peyton shut his eyes and took in a deep breath. "If this is the part where you pull your gun and threaten me, let's do it quick. I'm fading."

"Nope. You already almost died. You get the point. That was a newbie move going there by yourself, but you had the right instincts. You were watching my back, and I appreciate it. Next time just lay the trail down and leave the ass-kicking to me, okay?"

Peyton groaned. "Yeah, no problem."

"We still have to deal with the aftermath, though. Now

he knows you're linked to Aletheia." Shay sighed. "I don't want to kill Weiss if I can avoid it."

"You don't have to. He doesn't know I'm linked to anyone."

Shay furrowed her brow. "You left out parts."

Peyton managed a weak grin. "He thinks I'm a freshman tomb raider who wanted to jump your claim. I made him think you were going after an artifact underneath a Walmart."

Shay let out a hearty laugh. "That proves you do listen to me. Still, keep your face out of the public. He might come after you again."

"Yeah. Hey, thanks for the assist with the doc and not dumping me in a ditch somewhere."

"You're an asset, a valuable one. Get some rest."

Peyton closed his eyes and let out a puff of air as his body finally relaxed.

Loyalty. That's what Peyton's actions proved. It would have been simple to sell her out while she was out of the country. He could have even appealed to the other tomb raider to take him on or Peyton could have tried his own hand at disappearing.

He was out working for the business.

Shay sighed as she left the room. Friends and loyalty. It will all take a little time to fit it into some kind of idea of new normal.

She still wasn't ready to tell Peyton that she'd disabled his dead man's switch.

Keep that piece of information close for now.

16

S hay stepped into the sprawling indoor Grand Central Market. People choked the narrow paths between the stands. The bright neon of the signs announcing each vendor in the wide-open warehouse of a space brought a smile to Shay's face, even if the large crowd size and bright lights all presented tactical threats.

Too many potential killers. Too many potential places to hide cameras and guns.

That didn't stop her stomach from rumbling.

"I think I'm feeling in a barbecue mood." She craned her neck looking around at the different places.

Damn it. Did I just say that? Please don't ask why, Peyton. Please don't ask.

Peyton eyed her. "Barbecue? Not pizza?"

Of course you noticed. Bastard.

"I eat other things. Like I said, I'm just in a barbecue mood."

"But I thought this was supposed to be our big post-job

meal. We always have pizza, and I don't think I've seen you eat barbecue since you rescued me."

Shay covered the slip up with a smile. "The only way to grow is to always try and vary your experiences, right? I don't have a special reason. It just sounds good to me right now."

Peyton shrugged. "Whatevah…"

Even as she offered her excuse, Brownstone's face popped into her mind. He'd asked her about barbecue. It was one of the few truly personal moments they shared when they'd worked together.

I'm trying to get into Brownstone's head by eating some barbecue. She rolled her eyes and cleared her throat. *Not like my pizza choices tell you much.*

Time to change the course of the conversation. "What do you want?"

"I think some tacos from Ana Maria's."

"Okay, grab some tacos, and I'll meet you at the front. We can eat at one of the outside tables."

The pair split apart, and Shay maneuvered through the crowds to grab some ribs to-go. She made a mental note of everyone she passed. Their clothes, the way they walked, any suspicious bulges, or if they seemed to be looking for someone or nervous.

She was in full blend mode with her Erdrem sheath dress and flats. The best way to not stand out in L.A. was to dress well. That would get you unnoticed in ninety percent of most situations.

Shay kept a small touch on every outfit to reflect her personality. A subtle but dark twist here and there, whether it was a glitter skull on her workout shirt or the small silver dagger pin decorating her dress.

Shay almost laughed as Peyton easily disappeared into the crowd. *there is more than one way to hide.*

He didn't do high end, not really, even with his current outfit of seersucker shorts with matching t-shirt by Desiigner. The ensemble worked in a casual California kind of way. Eclectic and functional.

Ten minutes later, Shay and Peyton found each other at the front of the market. She nodded to him as they headed out to one of the large red metal tables lining the street in front of the market.

They ate a few bites of their meals in silence. Shay continued to watch the flow of traffic, both people and cars. Eating outdoors in the line of sight of so many windows violated every decent principle of defensive seating, but it was still good practice. She couldn't always control her situation.

Peyton gestured to a tall apartment building around the corner. "Grand Central Square Apartments. I should get a place there. Great access to this place and a bunch of other cool amenities. Pool, dry cleaners, women. I could get a dog."

Shay shook her head. "It's not defensible. Way too much traffic. Too hard to see who might be watching. I could take someone out in one of those apartments a variety of ways without even going inside."

Peyton furrowed his brow and continued to stare at the apartments. She could tell that he was trying to figure out a way to make it work.

Shay finished polishing off a rib and wiped her hands on a napkin. "Not gonna happen. I'm impressed you didn't end up dead when I was gone, but you still have to prove you're learning something about this business and know the smart moves. I'm not convinced of that, not by a long shot."

As much as she respected him going the extra mile to verify he'd fooled Weiss, he'd been sloppy about it. He made it too easy for the other tomb raider to catch him, and he ended up poisoned. If Shay had been a few hours later, Peyton would be already buried.

Shay would have verified Weiss' presence from miles away or using a drone. Peyton was still eager, too green, and if he were going to survive, he needed to learn that bravery and loyalty weren't enough, not by themselves at least.

Peyton didn't say anything until he finished off his tacos. "There was another place I've been looking at. We can check it out, and you can tell me what you think. It's in a less crowded area."

"I'll check it, but that doesn't mean I'll agree."

"Doesn't hurt to look at it, though." Peyton winked, brushing off the front of his shirt.

"Nice loft apartment, huh?" Peyton's eyes were full of expectant joy. "Not that far from the beach, either. And Manhattan Beach is a calm neighborhood full of young families. I like the idea of living *somewhere* with Manhattan in the name."

Shay shook her head. Loft apartment was a stretch. It

was a jumped-up converted garage. She didn't get why he was so into the place.

Peyton hurried over to the door and opened the top half. "Check that out. I love Dutch doors. Lots of places around here have them. I can keep it open and smell the ocean from here. Even sit outside with coffee in the morning."

"The ocean just smells like salt. And this place has absolutely no security. The lock wouldn't keep out the average burglar. That walkway in front of your place extends for miles."

"Yep. To a lot of different neighborhoods like Redondo and Hermosa Beach."

Shay wrinkled her forehead, shaking her head. "That's not a good thing. It means it's easy access in and out of your place. I'm not convinced this is much better than the warehouse, anyway."

It also didn't help that the place wasn't close to any of her warehouses, and no top-tier pizza places nearby. Even if Peyton didn't care about that sort of thing, that didn't mean Shay could ignore the fundamentals.

Peyton rolled his eyes, crossing his arms over his chest. "Yeah, because living in an office with cameras everywhere and cubicle walls is totally the same as having my own place."

Shay pointed at the door. "I could break in here and you wouldn't even be awake before I slit your throat. If I can do it, there are other killers who can do it."

"Point. Here's a counter-point. This is the kind of neighborhood where people who don't belong stand out, and because people here actually have money, they are likely to call the cops. This isn't some squeezy industrial zone full of nothing but bums and warehouses."

Shay snorted. "The police are always minutes away when seconds count. If you're depending on the cops to save your ass from a hitman, you might as well blow out your own brains now."

"Come on. I'm not an idiot, Shay." Peyton pointed at the different corners of the room and the windows. "I'm going to up the security on this place. Sensors on all the windows and doors. Cameras. There are enough drones around already that I can set up my own automatic surveillance drone, and no one will pay it any attention. Add a few gadgets and traps, and this place, if anything, will be *more* secure than the warehouse."

"It's your life to gamble." Shay shrugged. "And if you get killed here, at least it doesn't mean someone's broken into the warehouse. Works out for me either way."

Peyton laughed. "I speak Shay talk. I know that means you care."

"I'm trying to keep you safe, but if you're hellbent on leaving I won't stop you. I get that you're smart enough to find a way to do things your way. Like the Walmart caper."

"I did that for you."

Shay held up her hand. "I know, whatever. The point is, you want this place, you get this place, but if you don't get those security upgrades in, you'll end up dead at the hands of a hitman."

Peyton shrugged. "Not all of us live next to cartel stash houses."

Shay grinned. "I don't. Not anymore at least." She nodded toward the door. "You do the paperwork, I'll help you move some of your shit over. Welcome back to independent living, Peyton."

———

Later that night, Peyton relaxed in his lounge chair, the only piece of furniture in the living room for the moment. Decorating would have to wait until he secured everything. Just because he wasn't as paranoid as Shay didn't mean he was carefree, and now he had at least two men who wanted him dead, his brother and Johann Weiss.

Something scratched at the door, and bile rose in the back of his throat.

Shit. I better not get killed my first night alone. Shay'll probably call me back as a ghost just to talk shit to me.

Peyton headed into the bedroom to pull out the pistol Shay had given him. He tucked it into the back of his waistband then looked through the peephole. Nothing.

Invisibility magic?

The scratching continued. Peyton swallowed, counted to three, and threw open the door. "Who's there?"

No zombie or rampaging Oriceran monster waited on the other side. There wasn't even the most banal of threats, like an L.A. gangbanger.

The source of the disturbing noise was a small orange tabby.

I almost wet myself over a cat. Nice. Yeah, so badass.

Peyton knelt. The animal's lack of collar and matted fur suggested a stray. The cat purred and rubbed against his hand.

"Don't have much to give you, but I think I can find a little snack."

The cat meowed.

Peyton smiled. "I need something to call you. How about Osiris?"

The cat meowed again, which Peyton took as confirmation that at least he didn't hate the name.

Look, Shay, not dead yet, and now I have a pet. Sort of. Everything's looking up.

17

Shay maneuvered through the thick crowd in the Leanan Sídhe. It was always jampacked with people.

Her own preferences about meeting places filled with fewer potential troublemakers didn't carry much weight with the Professor. The man made it clear that he'd hand out assignments at the Irish pub, and nowhere else.

He'd reached out to her online and quoted a rather hefty payment amount as bait. Money was a strong motivator and key to her current life plan of sustainable and safe retirement.

He feels safe here. The security arrangements the owners have must be secure if a man like the Professor has no problem arranging for pretty serious jobs here. Someday he'll tell me.

The Professor sat in a booth near the back, sipping on some beer. He waved to Shay, and she gave him a polite nod back before making her way to him.

"A wonderful evening, isn't it, Miss Carson?"

Shay slid into the booth and glanced at the menu even

though she wasn't here for the food. "The smog count is low. I'll take it as a win."

"Get a few more beers in you, and I suspect you'll find it as wonderful as I do. Life's always better when you don't take it so seriously."

The Professor's red cheeks weren't all that different than normal, but she still found herself questioning how much the alcohol even affected the man. His Father O'Banion persona seemed more out of control, but Shay couldn't shake the feeling that the man was manipulating people with his drunken image.

"I'm not really here to drink. I'm here because I've heard you have a job for me, and I'm a greedy woman who loves money." Shay smirked.

"Aye, I do. I was very satisfied with your Peruvian performance, and so I'm interested in you gathering something else for me. It's a somewhat time-sensitive matter, which is why I've asked you directly rather than checking around."

Shay shrugged. "If the pay is right, I'll grab whatever you need as quickly as you need it."

The Professor smiled and gulped down some more beer. "Are you familiar with the Sree Padmanabhaswamy Temple in India?"

"Only that there are a number of vaults there, and they used to be filled with treasure. Jewels, coins, idols made of precious metals collected over the centuries. The works. They discovered several hidden vaults, too. I've heard some rumors though that they've opened even the hidden vaults and removed most of the treasure since the initial discoveries in the past couple decades."

A disappointed look spread over the man's face. "Aye, they have. There was no way they could leave all that treasure in there when people were already finding ways inside, including hidden tunnels. Most of the precious objects not used in rituals have already been relocated to protect them from thieves."

Shay furrowed her brow. "But not all of the treasure? That's the job? The left-over treasure?"

"Oh, I'm not interested jewels and gold. I've access to more money than I could ever drink, and I can drink a lot."

"You're saying there's an artifact inside?"

The Professor nodded. "It's come to my attention that technology is insufficient to uncover all the vaults in the temple. There is yet another hidden vault that is... Well, the best way to explain it is to note that it's folded atop the existing space magically. That is there are two vaults occupying one space."

"That's different. Sounds kind of annoying for the architect."

The Professor chuckled, shaking a finger at her. "Aye."

"And how does a woman, say your friendly greedy tomb raider, get to said second vault, then?"

"To access the other vault, you'll need another artifact. A flute."

Shay blew out a breath. This was already getting way more complicated than the Peru job. "A flute? That's... different. Okay, any line on the thing? Or is this a two-part deal?"

The man grinned. "Oh, that's not an issue. I already have the flute, and I'm more than happy to loan it to you."

The Professor let out a quiet chuckle. "Just don't lose it, Miss Carson. It's rather valuable."

Shay snorted. "I'm not the kind of woman who loses things, especially artifacts."

"No, I suppose you're not." The Professor drained the last of his beer. "You shouldn't use the flute until you get to the first vault."

"How does it work? I don't know how to play any type of flute. If it needs a specific tune, I'm screwed."

"It's not so complicated. Just blow on it. Well, you could try and use it before, but you'll end up dead." The Professor shrugged. "Don't do that, please. You're too pretty to die so young."

Shay nodded. "Okay, duly noted."

"I'll need you to infiltrate the hidden tunnels beneath the main temple, make your way to the hidden vault, and then use the flute to transfer yourself to the target vault. I even have a perfect route for you to take. Once you agree to the job, I'll share the information with you."

Shay nodded. "Seems simple enough, but I'm not gonna lie. I'm surprised you're offering me a job like this."

The Professor's eyebrows rose. "Surprised?"

"That place is still active and in use. This isn't tomb raiding. It's more like…"

"Robbery?"

Shay shrugged easily. She knew some killers for hire wouldn't steal a dime. In tomb raiding she found it to be a grey area. "I'm not saying I won't do it, but this sort of thing doesn't strike me as your style."

The Professor glanced to his side as a waitress

approached with another glass of beer. She set it in front of the man.

They knew him so well at the pub he didn't even have to ask for a refill. He was personally responsible for the owner's kids being able to afford the better summer camp.

Smite-Williams swallowed down most of his new drink. "You're right, Miss Carson. Normally, I wouldn't ask for someone to take something already being guarded in a sense, but there is an object inside that vault that is too dangerous to be left where it is. My flute isn't the only way to find the final vault, and the temple's security has always been lackluster."

The Professor sighed. "Which is why they had to remove the gold and jewels inside of the hidden vaults. I have zero confidence they can defend an artifact they likely don't even know is inside their temple."

"What's inside that's such a big deal?"

"A small figurine depicting the four-armed blue-skinned form of the god Vishnu sleeping atop a golden serpent, specifically, Adishesha, the King of all Nagas." The Professor furrowed his brow. "Are you familiar with nagas?"

"Snake beings, right? Not evil inherently, or anything, but more powerful than humans, and some were just as cruel and dangerous as us. They were particularly known for fucking with humans who mess with areas they protect. At least that's what legend says."

The Professor shrugged. "Yes. The return of magic has awoken some of the surviving nagas, but most don't interact with humans from what I understand."

"Great. Magical snake creatures might be guarding this temple?"

An odd look crossed his face for a moment. "No, there are no nagas in the temple. There shouldn't be at least."

She didn't like the use of the phrase "at least."

"Okay." Shay frowned. "What are you getting at? Don't hold back on me."

"There shouldn't be any nagas there, but if there are, they will try and kill you. You don't need to exercise restraint against them."

"You're saying some nagas are looking for this figurine?"

"Perhaps, if not now, they will be sooner rather than later. That's why it's important to get our hands on it now."

Frog dudes and now snake men? Kind of missing the Warlocks now. They almost seem tame in comparison.

"What's the big deal about some figurine? I get that it's magic, but what does it do?" Shay held up her hand to catch the waitress. Might as well drink a beer and keep him company. Not that he was asking.

A huge smile appeared on the older man's face. "What would you say if I told you, you didn't need to know?"

"I'd say you can take your money and stuff it up your ass."

Shay held her breath, realizing she might have gone too far.

The Professor burst out laughing and slapped a hand on his knee. "Aye, that'd be a good response."

Shay spread her hands out on the table, relieved as she let out the breath. "When my life's on the line, I need to have all the relevant information."

"It's a key, Miss Carson. It has the potential to control a vimana."

"You mean one of those old-school Hindu god chariots?"

"Some are associated with the ancient gods, yes. A true vimana is much more than a chariot. In this case, think more like a flying magical palace with magical weaponry. The descriptions in epics like the *Ramayana* are not to be dismissed as mere myth."

Shay stared at the Professor for a good ten seconds before talking. "Are you saying you have a flying castle parked somewhere, Professor?"

"Not on this planet." He smiled as he took another drink. "You're only being tasked with finding the key. That is information you don't need to know one way or another. Let me say, though, that sometimes the best way to stop a drunk driver is take away his keys." He winked and raised his glass.

"You're the drunkest person I know and apparently lack irony."

"Then it should terrify you that I'm worried about someone else."

Even with all the wonders and terrors of magic that had returned to the world, Shay found it hard to believe that anyone might be flying around a magical palace, but hard to believe wasn't the same thing as impossible.

It also didn't matter what she believed. The Professor was willing to pay her a lot of money to get a figurine. Shay believed in what money could buy, for sure.

"You're paying me a lot for this job. A lot more than you did for the Peru job. Makes me think you do have the vimana tucked under a lake somewhere or hidden in an arctic Fortress of Alcohol."

"Perhaps, Miss Carson, but in truth, the premium for the job is for a far different reason. One you already highlighted."

Shay furrowed her brow, not liking the confusion settling over her. "What are you getting at?"

"The temple is in use. This is a theft of sorts, even if a necessary one. I'm hoping the information I give you will allow you to recover the artifact without encountering resistance from innocent people."

Shay's stomach tightened. She didn't like where this conversation was going.

"And if I encounter resistance?"

"I'd strongly prefer if you didn't kill any humans. The people who control the temple might not be doing the best job in protecting all their treasures and artifacts, but they also aren't bad people, and don't deserve to be harmed by random tomb raiders."

Shay rubbed her temple as the waitress put a glass down in front of her. She waited till the waitress had walked far enough away and leaned in to whisper. "And what if they try to kill me?"

"Be creative. Use your sense of humor to distract them. Try some feminine wiles. I hear those are still in vogue. Whatever it takes. Just no killing of innocents."

Shay smirked. "How would you even know if I killed anyone, innocent or otherwise?"

An amused glint appeared in his eyes. "Oh, I have my ways. Though I have a more practical solution that will help you, should you encounter not-so-innocent resistance."

"What?"

The Professor held up a hand while he took another sip. "There are plenty of bounties in the city hosting the temple and the surrounding state. It'd be easy enough to get James to go with you…"

"No," Shay snapped.

The Professor's brow rose. "No?"

"No Brownstone on this one. From what you told me, I'm going to be avoiding people, and you don't expect magical trouble. That means the chance of a problem I can't handle is low. I don't need a babysitter, let alone a big-ass one. Let's not make it a habit."

"And what if I said I insisted?"

"I'd say you can find yourself another tomb raider." Shay gave him a thin smile. "And you're the one on a tight schedule."

She didn't object to the idea of Brownstone. She knew the man could kick ass and keep it professional, but she also needed to make the Professor understand she didn't always want someone else tagging along. Getting too used to the man would be a bad habit.

Having barbecue with him and heading out to help with Harriken meant she was already opening herself up to the dangerous man way too much.

"Very well, Miss Carson. Fair enough. I won't force you to take James this time. But be aware that doesn't mean I won't ask again. And I may very well insist next time."

Shay nodded as she took a long drink from the cold

beer and set the glass down. "Case-by-case basis. Fine by me."

She resisted adding Brownstone might be busy dealing with the Harriken. They might not leave him alone. After what he'd done, it'd make sense if they did, but honor-obsessed criminals weren't always rational.

The Professor smiled. "I'll forward you the relevant information about the layout of the tunnel system. Call me before you set out for the airport. I'll have a courier deliver you the flute there. Oh, I should warn you. When you use the flute, there will be some momentary discomfort."

"I'm sure I can handle it."

"Do we have a deal, Miss Carson?"

"Don't worry, Smite-Williams. I'll get you your magical flying palace key."

"Definitely hard to miss," Shay whispered.

The one-hundred-foot, seven-tier gatehouse tower to the temple rose above the nearby simpler buildings of the city of Thiruvananthapuram. Elaborate depictions of gods, warriors, and couples sat carved into the stone. If the intricate stonework wasn't sufficient to impress, the gold-plating over the tower would do the rest.

The various people wandering the streets nearby didn't seem to take any special notice of the temple. They had stopped being impressed a long time ago.

Too bad. I'm not going to see most of it.

Fencing and walls surrounded the outer ramparts of the temple complex, their steel contrasting with the older stone. The rise in thefts had led to a greater emphasis on security.

Don't worry. I don't want any of the gold, guys, just your little figurine. If the Professor's right, you don't even know it's there.

Shay took a deep breath. It was time to head back to her hotel room and rest for a bit. The job would start well after nightfall.

She wasn't there for sightseeing, and she didn't need any witnesses.

A helpful EMP disabled the nearby streetlights as Shay crept through the darkness. Few people prowled the streets near Padmatheertham, the large pond dominating the area right outside of the temple complex.

Shay didn't want to have to explain to any random passersby why she was wearing a wetsuit. The Professor's information said the safest way into the hidden tunnels involved a hidden underwater passage.

Shit. If this takes until sun up, I'll have to sit inside the temple for a while. Or find a new way out.

Shay found a small grove of trees near a corner of the rectangular pond. She slipped on a diving mask and head-lamp before connecting a small water-tight bag to her belt.

The bag contained the key things she'd need once she was out of the water. Inside were a gun, a few magazines, the temporary knives from Tubal-Cain, a folded up tactical harness, her phone, her smartwatch, and some boots.

Boots and a wetsuit. Oh so fashionable.

Shay snickered, knowing this kind of entry wasn't happening with Brownstone.

See, Smite-Williams? Sometimes two people are a crowd.

She lifted her final tool. A tankless rebreather. She bit down on the mouthpiece and leapt into the water.

Shay didn't like using the device. The batteries didn't last long, and it was worthless at any decent depth, but she wouldn't need to be in the water long or go deep. Her only other option involved trying to sneak a bunch of SCUBA gear into the middle of the city, difficult even at night.

She turned on her headlamp. The beam cut through the inky blackness of the water as she made her way toward the other side of the pond. The algae-covered stone wall closed on her, and she stopped swimming.

Her light passed back and forth over the wall as she sought evidence of the hidden tunnel.

Damn it. Not gonna be that easy. Okay, let's do this the hard way.

Shay swam toward the wall and ran her hands along the stone. Her heart thumped as the minutes passed. She needed enough oxygen to get to the temple and back if she didn't want to deal with further complications.

Five minutes passed when her hand pushed into the wall. Shay's eyes widened as she stared down at her arm.

It was if the wall swallowed her hand, but she didn't feel anything other than more water. A quick exploration with both hands revealed a circular tunnel behind the apparent wall. She wasn't sure if it was technology, clever lighting, or magic giving the appearance of an otherwise solid wall.

Next time they drain this thing, they'll probably find this tunnel. All right, here we go.

Shay swam forward. Her head passed through the fake wall, and her headlamp revealed a smooth if narrow tunnel stretching out ahead of her. She kept moving forward until her light illuminated another wall ahead.

Shay changed directions, swimming up along the wall

until her head popped out of the water in a small earthen chamber. The dirt and rock covered floor and jagged and irregular walls meant it wasn't part of the main temple complex.

Shay ditched her rebreather and mask before slipping on her boots and harness. The gun and knives joined her outfit next before she put on her watch and her phone in a harness pouch. The implications of the light loadout didn't escape her. If Shay ended in a major battle, she would be screwed.

But I'm not supposed to kill anyone anyway. Right, Professor?

She took a moment to check a pouch for the Professor's small wooden flute. The warm to the touch instrument remained where she'd left it.

A step outside the chamber brought her to a wide but irregular tunnel. Shay hurried down the tunnel, the head-lamp beam revealing nothing but more dirt and darkness. Ten minutes of travel brought her to a fork in the path.

She pulled out her phone to check the custom map app Peyton had uploaded her information into.

Glad I wasn't trying to depend on getting a signal in the ground under a temple.

Peyton's research and hacking retrieved subterranean density maps derived from data gathered by a government geological survey plane. She'd found they were more up-to-date than most of the map information the Professor provided.

What interested Shay most was this information revealed that at least someone was aware of how extensive the tunnel system was underneath the temple.

They'd made a rookie mistake in terms of security. They should have collapsed most, if not all, of the tunnels. Going through a door would always be easier than digging through the ground.

Her navigation through the mazelike tunnels brought her to her destination. A gilded golden door covered with an elaborate carving of Vishnu. She pulled on the huge handle, straining with a grunt.

Inside the cavernous stone chamber, piles of gold, golden idols, and jewels littered the low-ceilinged chamber inside. They glinted under the light of her headlamp.

"And I thought they'd taken all this stuff out already, Professor. Even you don't always have all the info, huh?"

Shay stepped inside the room and eyed the contents. Bulky and hard to carry. That was the problem with most conventional treasure and why she'd focused her career on magical items.

She reached into her pouch to pull out the flute. "Hope this shit works." She blew in it once. No sound emerged. She blew in it again.

Okay, that was anti-climatic.

A few seconds later, Shay collapsed to her knees as vertigo overwhelmed her. The world around her twisted in on itself, the colors blurring and shifting.

"Fuck." Her dinner threatened to come up.

A few careful, deep breaths followed. The room continued to twist and shudder, with two sets of walls passing through each other as if they didn't exist to each other. She tried to focus, but the entire room stubbornly refused to return to anything normal. Her pulse pounded in her ears and pain spiked in her head.

A tiny painted clay figurine of Vishnu resting atop the serpent sat in the corner, the only new object inside the room she could make out in the mess.

The key. Smaller than I expected.

Shay crawled over toward the figurine. Her stomach churned, and bile rose in her throat. She grabbed the figurine, shoved the flute to her mouth, and blew again.

The world returned to normal, even if her breathing remained ragged.

What the fuck? You call that momentary discomfort, Smite-Williams?

Shay lay on her back, staring up at the cracked stone ceiling above her. The cold figurine rested in the palm of her hand.

"That wasn't fun."

She let a few more minutes pass for her stomach and heart to settle before standing up and slipping the figurine into a pouch.

Peyton's information combined with the Professor's eliminated aimless wandering. She'd made excellent time and could escape the temple well before she lost the cover of night outside.

Her footsteps echoed in the tunnels as she walked back toward the water entrance. The trip gave her time to reflect on how things had changed for her.

I wasn't sure if Peyton would be a help, but damned if he hasn't been a big help. Can't admit it to the guy, but not so sure I'd already be doing jobs for people like Smite-Williams so quickly without his help.

Teamwork still weighed on her heart and filled her

with doubt. The line between her being self-reliant and dependent blurred with each job.

Is it a good thing? I don't know. Maybe it's not a totally stupid thing to have someone like Brownstone having my back on jobs like this. It's not I can't do this shit by myself, just makes it easier.

Shay continued down the tunnel and let out a quiet sigh. At least she didn't need Brownstone after this job. She'd not so much as seen a shadow of anyone.

A second after the thought left her head, a barefoot Indian man in a thin dark robe stepped around a corner, frowning.

Shay stopped, convinced the man was a trick of the light.

The man narrowed his eyes and crossed his arms. The robe didn't match the pattern or brighter colors of the other men she'd spotted when surveilling the temple earlier in the day, but she wasn't an expert on Indian religious clothing.

Shay sucked in a deep breath as she thought over her next move. Her instinct was to pull her gun and shoot the man down, but she didn't doubt the Professor possessed some way of telling if she did just that, and she couldn't risk losing a high-profile client.

Not only that, but killing some random man for being at the wrong place at the wrong time struck her as a little unfair. She might have been a killer, but she wasn't a random murderer or a complete dick like the Harriken.

He's some dude in a temple. All it'll take is a little intimidation.

Shay pulled out her pistol. "Turn around, put your hands behind your head, and you don't have to die."

"No," the man responded.

"You don't have to die here, pal. I don't want to kill you. Seriously."

The man tilted his head to the side. "I can see it. Its power glows."

Fuck. This is going south already.

"I don't know what you're talking about," Shay said.

"You think I'm a fool? You think I believe you've entered this temple with honorable intentions?"

Shay barked out a laugh. "Not saying I did, but also I'm leaving. So either come at me, or get the fuck out of my way. I don't..."

She narrowed her eyes and stared at the man. The tunnels were pitch black without a light source. She'd been relying on her headlamp.

The man carried no torch, flashlight, or lamp. He wasn't even wearing shoes, let alone AR goggles. If he could see in the dark, that meant he wasn't a normal man.

Fuck, Professor. Thanks for the total lack of warning about magical temple guardians.

Shay lifted her pistol. "Get the fuck out of my way right now. I'm done playing around."

"Human garbage," the man said. He spit on the ground. "You infest this country. You infest this planet. You're nothing. A mistake. You make a mockery of the *dharma.*"

"I make a mockery out of a lot of stuff, but I'm pretty sure anyone holy thinks I'm bad news." Shay waved the gun a few times. "This is your last chance."

"Give me the heart. I can see its glow on you. Humans should not pollute a vimana."

So he knows I have the vimana key, huh?

"I don't have time for this shit." Shay pointed her gun at his head.

"Give me the heart, or I will make your death agonizingly slow as I consume you."

"See, this is where I'm nicer, because... What the fuck did you just say? Consume me?"

The man took a step forward and blinked. When his lids lifted, the brown human eyes were gone, replaced by slitted pupils surrounded by emerald green.

Not human? That makes this easy .

Shay put three rounds into the naga's head. He stumbled back, and she waited for him to fall.

He never did.

His human body contorted, twisted, and grew, his skin hardening and scales appearing.

Shay stumbled backward, holstering her pistol and pulling out one of Tubal-Cain's temporary knives.

The entire transformation from man to human-sized cobra took only seconds. The naga hissed, its head bobbing from side to side.

Shay waited, her grip around the knife tight. A viscous liquid dripped from the fangs of the creature, and she didn't want to test if it was venomous.

Her enemy surged forward and snapped at her. Shay spun, leaving only air for the naga's fangs. She slashed with the blade. Yellow blood spurted from the wound.

A knife shouldn't have worked when a gun didn't, but

she wasn't about to question a decent hit. Maybe the gnome's craftmanship was even better than she expected.

Shay leapt back in time to avoid her enemy's counterattack. He snapped again at her, but she backed up to avoid the blow.

Damn it. Need something to block this asshole with.

Their entire battle had only been under a minute, but the naga's wound had already started to close. She needed to slow the damned snake down somehow.

The naga whipped its tail. It connected with Shay, sending her slamming into a wall with a hiss of pain. His follow-up attack with his fangs missed her by inches. Not that the fact made her ribs feel any better.

This is what I get for not bringing some grenades.

Shay yanked out another knife and took a few swings. The naga jerked underneath her weapon.

"So you are afraid, huh? Yeah, these are just loaners. Wait until I get the real deal. I'll be skinning all sorts of snakes to make boots out of."

Human and snake both got in a few good hits. The naga was bleeding all over now, and even though he'd not managed to hit Shay with his fangs, his powerful tail ensured she'd have more than a few bruises on her way home, if not broken bones judging by the ache.

I need to end this shit.

The naga slid forward and struck at Shay, as if he could sense her concern. His fangs ripped a tear in the arm of her wetsuit but didn't meet flesh. Ignoring her pounding heart, Shay jammed the knife in her offhand into the head of her enemy.

He thrashed and hissed. Shay followed with a series of

quick stabs with both weapons. The naga's head fell to the ground, and she dropped, letting the force of gravity aid her in piercing through the creature's head with her first knife. Her blade stuck in the ground, pinning the giant snake.

The naga continued to twitch, and Shay slammed the other knife through its head. She readied her third knife and hacked and slashed away at its neck until she separated it from the body.

Shay sat there, covered in yellow blood, her breathing ragged.

This is the difference between a killer and an assassin. A real killer is already ready to finish up close.

She removed the knives and sheathed them before kicking the head away from the body, unsure if the creature could still regenerate after being decapitated.

"Told you to get the fuck out of my way, snakeboy."

Shay sprinted into the darkness.

These are some nice fucking knives. Better get that adamantine sooner than later.

19

Shay stretched and stifled a yawn as she scrolled through some spreadsheets on her desk computer.

Even on the fastest commercial supersonic flight available, it'd taken a decent trip to get back to Los Angeles. Still, the key was out of her hands and with the Professor, no nagas had shown up to kill her, and Peyton managed not to get assassinated while she was in India.

She was also now millions of dollars richer. Sure, the naga had banged her up a bit, but a quick trip to Doctor Chao confirmed nothing was broken.

Shay's phone rang. She glanced down at the caller ID.

Brownstone managed not to die while I was gone. How many massacres did he rack up? And I thought I didn't take shit from anyone.

Shay snickered and answered the phone. "Brownstone, to what do I owe the pleasure?"

"I need your help with something if you have some time."

Probably not time to steam up the sheets, though, huh?

Shay blew out a breath. "Does this involve killing houses full of gangsters again?"

"Not today, I don't think."

"I love the implied promise." Shay chuckled. "What's up?"

"This is related to the Harriken, just not killing them. Yet."

Shay wasn't sure if she should be getting in so deep with the man, but she'd already been prepared to help the first time, so it didn't seem a stretch to consider helping him a second time. Killing the man's dog was an asshole move, and so the gangsters would get what was coming to them.

"Okay, I'm listening."

"I originally got the attention of the Harriken because I rescued a teenage girl from two guys trying to snatch her. She was looking for her mom."

Really, Brownstone? I thought you were Mr. Total Bounty Hunter, but you're running around saving teens from traffickers? You're more of a softy than I thought.

For some reason, the thought comforted Shay, but she didn't want to show the man any emotional weakness.

"Yeah, and?" she said. "That sounds like every Tuesday in L.A."

"Well, I've got that girl with me now. Turns out her dad was the one who sold her mom to the Harriken."

Okay, so there's someone from a far more fucked-up family than even mine.

"Huh, that's different," Shay said. "Kidnapping a middle-aged mother to turn her into a prostitute or something seems tailor-made to bring down trouble on you, bounty hunter…or the law."

"There's something more here. Not sure what, but first things first. I wanted to know if you could watch her for a bit while I talk to some people about taking care of her."

"Why me?" Shay asked.

She prayed her voice didn't betray her thumping heart. Brownstone trusted her enough that he wanted her help, rather than the other way around. It shouldn't have mattered so much, but she still liked it.

Brownstone grunted. "You showed up because you were pissed about a dog. I don't think you'd sell out a little girl, and I know you know how to use a gun. My other first-line choices include two hardcore drunks."

The explanation deflated Shay.

"So it was me or a drunk?"

"Yeah, something like that."

Shay snickered. "You need better friends, Brownstone."

"We all get the friends we deserve."

"Yeah, don't I know it, which is why my friends have tried to kill me," Shay muttered under her breath before speaking up. "Whatever. Okay, sure, I'll help, if it isn't for too long. I'm not a babysitter. I'm a field archaeologist."

What the fuck am I doing? Should I get Peyton involved? No, no. This is my shit. He needs to be insulated from it. I'm the one suddenly being a soft touch.

"Thanks," Brownstone said. "Meet me at my place. You guys can stay there. I don't think the Harriken will come sniffing around me directly for a while after my little demonstration."

I need to turn this to my advantage somehow, otherwise Brownstone will think I'm his bitch.

"Okay, Brownstone, I'll do this, but you owe me one."

He ended the call.

Shay rubbed her temples. "What the hell am I doing?"

After Shay knocked on Brownstone's door, she crossed her arms and started tapping her foot. Everything about this was idiotic. She couldn't figure out what weird hold Brownstone had over her that kept making her want to help him.

If she weren't already in the Harriken's sights for showing up at their house the night of the massacre, helping Brownstone protect one of their targets would put her square in the crosshairs.

If the Harrken start digging, other people might show up.

Still, earning a little trust and a favor from the bounty hunter might be worth it. Plus, she suspected the local Harriken population would nosedive over the next few days.

The door finally opened, revealing the barbecue-loving bounty hunter. He wore his leather jacket on his body and a concerned look on his face.

Brownstone gestured her inside. "Alison's on the couch." He pulled a key out of his pocket. "No reason for you to go anywhere, but just in case."

"Oh, giving me the key to your place already?" Shay winked.

Brownstone just stared at her until she shrugged and

sighed. For a man who liked to talk a lot of shit, he could be boring at times.

"I'll be back soon." He headed out the door. "I know you don't like spooky basements, but just so you know—the basement door is locked and sealed for a reason."

Shay glanced that way. "Because it's your Red Room of Pain?"

"It's booby-trapped, too." The bounty hunter shook his head and closed the door behind him.

"Well, at least it's not fucking Inca zombies this time," Shay muttered under her breath.

Or stupid naga.

She continued deeper into the house, taking in the carefully arranged furniture and neatly piled stacks of papers. She spotted Alison on the couch, her hands folded in her lap.

The girl looked up and offered her a smile. She tilted her head, staring at Shay without saying anything. The girl's eyes seemed unfocused, and something about her expression unsettled Shay.

Trauma maybe, from dealing with an asshole dad. Shay could understand that. It wasn't like she'd grown up with the best parents. They hadn't tried to sell her to gangsters, though—she had to give them that.

The field archaeologist reached up and brushed at her cheek. "What? Something on my face?"

"No. I mean, maybe."

"Maybe?"

"It's just that you kind of remind me of Mr. Brownstone."

"How?"

"A beautiful soul covered in a lot of pain."

Shay blinked several times, completely unsure how to respond to that. "Okay. Thanks for that. Whatever that means."

The girl rose and offered her hand. "I'm Alison, by the way. Alison Anderson." Her smile disappeared. "Though I think I should get my last name changed. I don't honestly know my mom's maiden name. I'll have to ask her once Mr. Brownstone gets her back."

"Yeah, I heard about your old man and your mom. Tough break." Shay shook the girl's hand. "I'm Shay. I'm a work associate of Brownstone's."

"You're a bounty hunter?" Disbelief colored Alison's voice.

Shay shook her head. "No, I specialize in freelance archaeology."

Alison's face scrunched in confusion. "Why would an archaeologist need to work with a bounty hunter?"

"You'd be surprised." Shay winked. "I'm kind of like a mix of Indiana Jones, Lara Croft, and Caleb Rodriguez."

"I've seen a few of the *Ancestor's Quest* movies, but I don't know who Indiana Jones and Lara Croft are."

Shay winced. It was the first time in her life she'd ever felt old, and she was only twenty-seven. Admittedly, she did have a predilection for the classic field archaeologist stories. They'd probably help inspire her second career choice along with her love of history.

"They are cooler than Caleb Rodriguez," she said. "I mean, he always uses so many drones and robots. It's just not the same as running from a boulder, watching Nazis melt, or punching sharks."

Alison shrugged. "If you say so."

Innocence clung to the girl in a way that almost turned Shay's stomach. Shay had been around Alison's age when she'd slid into a world of suffering and darkness. Maybe Brownstone could save the girl from a similar fate.

Shay returned her attention to the house. She ran her finger along a windowsill. No dust. *The man dusted his windowsills.* She didn't even do that.

"So have you known Mr. Brownstone long?" Alison asked.

"Nope. Just met him recently on a job."

"He's a good guy, you know. He's saved me twice from the Harriken."

"Yeah, he's okay for a guy."

So I was right before. So much for you only being in it for the money, Brownstone. Helping out little damsels in distress? Where's the profit in that?

A bookshelf caught Shay's attention. Closer inspection revealed three rows of books, the top being cookbooks and the bottom two all being books related to barbecue. History, cooking, chefs, and restaurants.

"The Case Against Molecular Gastronomy as Applied to Barbeque," Shay read. She shook her head. "Man, does this guy like his barbecue!"

Alison tilted her head to the side. "What?"

"Nothing, just... Brownstone's real OCD. I didn't expect that from a guy who... Well, a guy like him."

He's gonna get OCD shooting six guys in the face.

Shay turned around and headed to the bathroom to peek inside. Three hand towels hung from a towel rack, all perfectly aligned. The toilet glistened, pristine. The light scent of pine hung in the air.

The bathtub looked factory-new.

"The guy doesn't even have hard-water stains," she muttered. "I scrub the damn thing, and I *still* have hard-water stains."

Alison rose from the couch and walked over to the bathroom. "What are you doing?"

"We need to leave," Shay told her. "Now."

The teenager's eyes widened. "Are the Harriken coming?"

"No." Shay took a deep breath. "This place is just...too perfect. If we mess anything up, both of us may end up dead. I'm taking you to my place, where a little mess isn't the end of the world."

"Hey, kid." Shay changed lanes. "You hungry?"

Alison nodded. "Yeah, a little."

"You like pizza?"

The girl smiled. "Who doesn't like pizza?"

"Who indeed? It's way better than barbecue." Shay grinned.

Alison laughed.

Shay pulled through an intersection. A great place was not all that far away. A little pizza always made everything better. Before they hit the pizzeria though, she needed a few questions answered.

"What's your deal, kid?"

Alison looked Shay's way, her eyes unfocused. "My

deal?"

"I've watched you move. It's…odd."

"Odd?"

"There's something I don't know." Shay sighed. "Look, kid, not trying to be a bi…not trying to be a jerk, but it's just lately I've run into a lot of people who aren't what they seem, and so I'd rather know upfront. I don't care if you're a half-angel/half-nymph or whatever. Brownstone asked me to protect you, so I'll protect you."

Alison laughed. "I'm not Oriceran; I'm just blind."

Shay spared a glance the teen's way. "Shit. Seriously? How do you get around so well? Do you do that sonar tongue clicking thing or whatever?"

"No. Not entirely. I'm not Oriceran, but I am special. I can see the energy of souls."

"Huh. Didn't see that coming. But somehow I'm not surprised."

Shay didn't even think to question the revelation. If anything, it made a lot more of the situation make sense. There was no reason for the Harriken to be obsessed with some random girl and her mother otherwise.

Brownstone, you stumbled into some seriously strange shit, even for a guy who hunts magical criminals for a living.

The implications of someone being able to read her deepest essence didn't sit well with Shay. Her neck and shoulders tightened, as she imagined just how awful her soul looked to an innocent young girl.

"You can see into me, huh?" Shay said.

"Yes."

"I've done a lot of bad things in my life. Just because I'm trying to do something different probably doesn't change who I am inside. I have all my excuses, but I was already a terrible person by the time I was your age."

Knowing that she couldn't hide her soul loosened Shay's tongue. No point in putting on too many airs for the ultimate lie detector. It'd be pathetic.

"No, you've got it all wrong." Alison shook her head.

"I do?"

"It's like I told you earlier, a beautiful soul with a lot of pain, but there's more and more beautiful colors. It's like it's changing into something even more beautiful."

Shay sighed. "I don't know if people can really change, including me."

"I've seen light in almost everyone's soul." A soft smile appeared on her face. "Like I said, I can already see more beauty building in you since you first came into Mr. Brownstone's house, and there was a lot before."

Shay swallowed and kept her eyes locked on the road. She didn't even want to begin to parse what the girl's information might mean. She'd only stopped by to help Brownstone out because he'd asked. It didn't change who she was, not really.

Maybe everything changed when I got pissed over that dog dying.

"That might be true, kid." Shay sighed. "But keep in mind that people can change from good to bad just as easily as from bad to good."

"I know." The girl's voice grew quiet. "I've seen that, too."

Shay turned into a parking lot for the pizzeria. "One last thing you need to know before we get something to eat."

"What?"

"Flat-crust only. No stuffed crust. It's an abomination that should be packed up and sent off to Oriceran."

Alison laughed. All the discomfort washed away from her face. "Okay, Shay."

Shay thought over everything that had happened in recent months. Peyton didn't die at the end of her gun despite his dead man's switch and the implied threat. That must have meant something, as did deciding to help Brownstone, even if he didn't turn out to need it.

Even the naga encounter proved something. She'd not known he was a naga at first. The old Shay would have gunned down a witness like that without a second thought.

Shit. So I am changing? I just don't know if I'm changing into something better or weaker.

Maybe both.

20

What the fuck am I doing? This is stupid.

After pizza, Shay took Alison to her new brownstone. The security of the place, along with the just added panic room, made it safe enough from random sword-wielding gangsters. Shay couldn't bring herself to babysit an already safe teen when the real action was coming up.

She'd texted Peyton to ask him to do a quick dig on anything involving the Harriken. Whatever information he could provide might help.

Now she was parked outside the Brownstone's house thinking about going to war with an entire gang. And all for no money.

I let that girl get into my head too much.

Shay sighed and headed toward Brownstone's door. His big-ass F-350 parked in the driveway proved he was home. She hadn't texted ahead, almost afraid to not let her pure instincts guide her at this point.

She grabbed the handle of his door and pulled it open.

Brownstone stood in the hallway, his .45 pointed right at her.

Oh shit.

Shay threw her hands up. "Don't shoot, Brownstone. It's me."

The bounty hunter narrowed his eyes and eased off the trigger. He took a deep breath and holstered his sidearm. "Where the fuck is Alison?"

Fuck. It would have been polite to knock. Be embarrassing if the guy I'm trying to help is the one who took me out.

"At my place. It's safer anyway. I have locks, and security actually made this century. And a panic room."

"Why the hell aren't you with her?"

Shay shrugged. "Because you're gonna need my help with your next mass-murder spree, big guy."

"Your help?" he asked as he put his pistol back up, locking it into its holster.

She nodded. "Yeah. I know how this whole thing ends. The kid told me about how you're gonna 'persuade' the Harriken." Shay made air quotes at the word persuade. "And we all know that in Brownstone-speak that means you're gonna kill every last one of those motherfuckers."

He grunted. "I might not need to kill *all* of them." He scratched his cheek. "Just most of them."

Shay stared at him. "The point is, sure, you took out that Harriken house, but wherever they're holding the kid's mom is probably a higher-security location. And now they know you're coming. It's gonna be shoot-on-sight, snipers...magic, for all you know. Maybe one of those talking statues you're so worried about."

She remembered him discussing that in an earlier

conversation. Her own recent encounters with statues only fueled her concern.

Brownstone locked eyes with Shay. "What I did in that house isn't my full strength. I've still got a few tricks to show them. I don't need help. Especially *your* help."

She crossed her arms over her chest. "Can you see behind you, Brownstone?" Shay let out a dark chuckle. "Because that's what it's gonna take not to die. You didn't exactly escape unhurt last time. A bullet through the head or heart will kill even you, Brownstone. Now imagine a .50-cal sniper bullet. Even your skull isn't thick enough to stop that."

Stop being such a stubborn bitch. Huh. That must be how the Professor thinks about me.

Brownstone dropped into his recliner. "I don't need some tomb raider to grab the mom while I'm distracting a few guys. If that was your plan, give it up."

He slammed his fist into his palm and twisted it as he looked at her. "This is applied ass-kicking, and I'm the expert here. This isn't about sneaking around, it's about tearing some motherfuckers apart. These guys are an infestation, and I'll be the exterminator."

Shay walked farther into his living room and loomed over him as he sat in the chair. She was tired of him thinking she was just a pretty face with a knowledge of history.

"I've got skills, Brownstone. I'm still new at the field archaeology gig. It's not what I trained for all my life."

The bounty hunter snorted as he shook his head, but he eyed her. "Skills? What, like pole dancing?"

Shay's mouth dropped open. Anger coursed through

her. Her heart kicked into overdrive, and she resisted slamming her first into the smug prick's face.

Maybe the Harriken aren't gonna be the ones who kill you, motherfucker.

"*What the fuck did you just say?*" Shay spat, hands on her hips.

Brownstones put up a hand. "I know you had a tough life as a stripper or a prostitute or whatever before and I'm sorry for that, but having seen the dark side of people isn't the same thing as doing what I do. It's not enough just to be angry."

This whole fucking time that's what he's been thinking? So you noticed me, Brownstone, just in a different way, huh?

Shay's hands curled into fists. "Is that what you fucking think? That I was a stripper or a prostitute?"

Brownstone shrugged and waved at her. "Yeah. You're good looking, you've got issues with men, and you won't talk about your past. Plus, you thought I was gay because I'm not into you. I take it that doesn't happen often."

Fuck your assumptions, you damned barbecue freak. And fuck you.

Shay grit her teeth and looked away, uncurling her fists as she crossed her arms. "This is bullshit." She tried to keep her anger in check. "I shouldn't have to tell you crap about my past."

Alluding a little to her rough life to Alison was one thing. Giving specific details to Brownstone, especially when she wasn't 100 percent sure she couldn't trust him to turn her into the cops was a different thing.

His voice was stony. "You want to join the party, then I need to know you have the skills to earn an invitation. If you won't tell me about your past, I can't trust you to have my back."

Shay looked away.

Would he really turn me in? The fucker just murdered a shit ton of people without a bounty. His hands aren't so clean, either.

Brownstone pushed out of his chair and stood up to stare down at Shay. "Yeah, you're right. One of the Harriken at the house gave up a location. I didn't know what it was for at the time, but now I get it. It's where Alison's mom is. I'm gonna raid the place and rescue her. And you're also right that it's gonna be more dangerous than what happened at the house." He squared his shoulders. "So if you want in, fucking convince me. Otherwise, shut up and go watch the girl."

Shay's mouth twitched for several seconds, and her eyes dropped. She blew out a huge breath.

"Okay, Brownstone, you win. I'm gonna share my secret with you, although it's something I've tried to leave behind. Just...give me a few minutes to prepare myself."

Shay walked into the kitchen and made herself at home. She opened the refrigerator, unsurprised to see everything organized in neat little rows.

"Your house is too damn clean, Brownstone," she called over her shoulder. "Are you *sure* you're not gay?"

The bounty hunter growled from the living room, "I'm not fucking gay, all right? Get over yourself, already."

He keeps saying that, but I still don't buy it.

"Really? This place is too damn clean and organized for a straight guy's house. Whoa, Henry Weinhard Root Beer. I haven't had this in years. Best head on a root beer ever."

Shay let out a sigh. "You're just so..." She shrugged and

whispered, "Okay, you're not into dudes, but I'll find out your secret, Brownstone."

"If I *was* gay, it wouldn't be a secret. No shame in my game."

Shay resisted the urge to grab a root beer. Pulling one out would mess up the symmetry in the container, and Brownstone would probably stroke out when he saw that.

Instead, Shay slowly walked back into the living room and sat on the couch, folding her hands in front of her.

Brownstone stared at her. "This isn't about *my* secrets, Shay. It's about yours."

"First off, I was never a stripper or prostitute or anything in the sex trade." She shrugged.

The bounty hunter grunted but didn't say anything.

"Better description would be too hot from too young." Shay held his gaze, not looking away.

Brownstone's face softened.

"I'm not from L.A., you know. I'm from out east. When I was fifteen, I caught the eye of a guy in my neighborhood. Nice guy, good looking, also happened to be heavily involved in running dust. The Oriceran shit, not PCP."

Brownstone leaned forward, intent on her story.

"This guy was, you know, really into me. I'm not gonna lie, Brownstone…when you're hot *you* know it and the world does too, so I knew the effect I had on men and boys. I used it to my advantage." Shay shrugged. "When Captain Dust showed up and started buying me gifts, I figured it was no big deal. I'd string him along and then move on, because it wasn't like he could do anything to me. I was only fifteen, right?"

The dark-haired woman took a deep breath and slowly

blew it out. Very few people knew what she was about to tell Brownstone. She'd tried to leave her past behind, but it was like the universe wanted to slap her in the face and shake her until she admitted what she was. No one could run from their true nature, it seemed.

"One day I was riding around in Captain Dust's car. He'd taken me out to dinner. I was so impressed with him. Then he told me to suck him off, and I told him to fuck off."

Brownstone's face hardened. Shay had no doubt about what this man would have done.

Shay gave a long sigh. "He pulled me out of the car, slapped me around, and told me that he fucking owned me and he could do what he wanted. I told him to fuck off some more, and he threw me down and told me he was just gonna take what he wanted." She closed her eyes. "For a second, you know, I thought, 'why don't I just let him fuck me, then he'll stop hurting me,' and I told myself, no, I couldn't do that, because the minute I let one guy do what he wanted, the next guy would as well."

Brownstone nodded slowly but didn't otherwise interject.

"So I told Captain Dust there to get the fuck off or I'd kill him. You know what he did then?"

Shay waited this time. She wanted to hear Brownstone's voice. It'd help anchor her in the present. Her dark emotions swelled and threatened to overwhelm her.

"What did he do?" the bounty hunter asked on cue.

The dark memories continued to pound Shay's mind, and her nails dug into her palm. A few trickles of blood started.

"He pulled out his gun and handed it to me. He slapped me so hard my head bounced off the car, and he told me that I was a stupid little cunt who didn't have the balls to kill him. He said that some people had the killer instinct, and some people didn't. He said I would be his forever." Shay stared into the distance, the painful memories feeling as fresh as they had twelve years before. "So I took the gun and shot him right in his dick."

Brownstone blinked and grimaced.

Shay swallowed. "You have to understand, it felt good. Not because I'd shot someone, but because I'd taken control. That was what I hadn't had before. When I was flirting my way through life I'd thought I was in control, but I was really just someone else's toy."

"So you shot him in the dick and let him go to make your point?"

"Would you have?"

Brownstone grunted. "I think you know the answer to that."

"Yeah. I gave him a speech about how I was going to take control, how it wouldn't just be my looks pushing through life, it'd be my skills. I shot him until the gun ran out of bullets." Shay sucked in and blew out several deep breaths. "I got rid of the gun, and when people came around asking me if I knew anything, I told them I didn't know shit."

"So you got away with it? None of his friends came looking for you?"

Shay stood up and started pacing. "No, because they made the same mistake you did, Brownstone. They assumed some pretty little thing couldn't be lethal. That I'd make a better stripper or escort or something." She waved a hand. "What I realized after that was that I could kill people and not feel bad about it. That it made me feel powerful and in control, so it grew from there—a life of killing. I was good at it, and people were willing to pay me good money to do it."

"So you became an assassin?"

"No!" Shay gritted her teeth. "I was a killer; cold-blooded, methodical and efficient, but not an assassin. Assassins are pussies who can't be bothered to get blood on themselves. They shoot from a distance. I wanted the people I killed to *know* that I was the one taking their life, to know *I* had the power."

Brownstone's expression had turned stony. She wasn't sure if he was judging her, but she did find it hard to believe that a man who had killed so many people that week would think she'd crossed a moral line.

"But you're not working as a killer now," he replied. "You're trying to be a tomb raider. If you're so damn good at it, why leave? Why not continue icing people for a paycheck?"

Shay stopped pacing, crossed her arms, and sighed. "Well, one dark and stormy night..." She laughed bitterly. "Yeah, I know...cliché, but that was part of the problem. Let's just say one night it caught up with me—what I'd become. So I walked out of my house as it went up in flames and left my old city and life behind. Too many skeletons for them to be sure I wasn't one of the dead. It wasn't like I'd used my real name for work anyway."

"So you have the skills, I'll give you that, but are you sure you want to help me? If you're trying to walk away from killing, helping me mow down a bunch of Harriken won't exactly set you back on the path of pacifism."

There was no challenge in Brownstone's eyes, just curiosity.

Shay shook her head. "I'm not a killer anymore, but I'm not a pacifist either. I'm like you—I think some people deserve to die. Now I just want to make sure I'm only killing people like that."

The bounty hunter nodded toward the door. "Let's go. The longer we wait, the more reinforcements they'll have. First, though, I have to go pick up a few things at the warehouse."

21

Shay resisted a snort. She owned several full warehouses, and Brownstone was keeping his shit in a storage unit like he was some divorced dad still living in a long-stay hotel.

"Yeah, I'm so judging you, Mr. Big-Shot Bounty Hunter. I'd be embarrassed to keep my top-notch killing gear in a storage unit. Fuck, how do you know someone won't break into it?"

Her phone chimed, and she picked it up. It was text from Peyton.

Your Japanese friends have put out a call for additional help. Several different groups have answered.

The text didn't surprise her, but she doubted Brownstone would want to run away because of a few extra people to kill.

Shay drummed her finger on her leg. She wondered what Brownstone was retrieving from his warehouse. The man already maintained a sealed secret basement she presumed was filled with a lovely assortment of killing implements.

Movement inside caught her attention. Brownstone turned the corner, pulling two suitcases. He pulled a necklace out of his pocket, and removed his jacket and shirt.

Shay took a second to appreciate Brownstone's body and the ink on his arms. She couldn't complain about the view, but the man's decision to suddenly strip confused her. He slipped the amulet around his neck.

Brownstone grimaced as the necklace sank into his flesh until it was fully embedded, then slipped his shirt back on and grabbed the suitcases.

Shay blinked several times. *I knew you had some sort of magical shit...or is that like some super-secret tech?*

She whispered, her voice floating inside the cab of the truck, "Just who or what the hell are you, James Brownstone?"

They only shared a few brief comments about the Harriken during their travel to the Belmont House, the Harriken base, with Shay reinforcing it was a rescue mission. Brownstone might be good at kicking ass, but restraint didn't seem one of his strong points.

They'd be coming up to a dirt road that would lead them to their final location. It was as good a time as any to pass along her little tidbit.

"It's not gonna just be the Harriken there. They've got others helping them out. Hired muscle."

Brownstone glanced her way. "How do you know that?"

"I've got information and sources for this sort of thing." Even though she was willing to kill to help him, she still didn't want him knowing all her secrets, such as Peyton, not yet anyway. "When you're used to being a killer for hire, you end up plugged into the scumbag information networks."

The bounty hunter grunted. "Anyone who chooses to get between me and the Harriken chooses to die. Simple as that."

Shay snorted. "Yeah, I thought you'd say something like that. Just thought I'd pass it along."

"Thanks."

* * *

The thin dirt road split off from the highway about fifteen minutes from Belmont House. After about ten minutes on the road, Brownstone turned off and drove into a dense cluster of pines.

So, here it comes. I'm about to help wipe out an entire gangster house and a bunch of other people because they are after that girl and killed a guy's dog.

Don't know if that means I'm a better person than I used to be or a worse person. It's good to get some practice in.

"We'll hoof it from here," Brownstone told her, shutting off the engine. "Otherwise, they may open up with an RPG or something as we drive up."

"Worried about dying right off the bat?" Shay teased.

"Nope, worried about losing this truck." He patted the dash. "I love this thing."

"Ah, yes...priorities. I'll try to make sure, as we lay

dying from getting shot a hundred times, that the Harriken promise not to fuck your truck up."

Brownstone grinned. "That would be handy."

Shay appreciated how laid back the man was as they prepared to go and mow down dozens of people. Nothing worse than an emotional and pissy killer.

They hopped out of the truck, and Brownstone pulled the suitcases from the back and unzipped them both. One contained boxes of ammo, along with guns and knives. The other contained various types of electronics, as well as a few tactical harnesses and holsters.

Shay leaned over to grab a harness, and spent a few moments tightening it while Brownstone fiddled with a black wristband.

"Jammer?" she asked. Brownstone was more prepared for all the possibilities than she'd thought.

He nodded. "Yeah. Long-range, but doesn't last all that long. I just want to make sure they don't sneak up on us with tactical drones. Too far from the city not to think they might have some of the heavier-duty shit. I prefer fighting people, not machines."

Finished with her harness, Shay eyed the weapons choices before grabbing a couple of semi-automatic pistols and a Steyr machine pistol. She spent the next few moments stuffing her harness with magazines. Efficiency in murder was always a good thing, but for a proper killing, a lady prepared herself for *all* eventualities.

The next few minutes passed in dead silence as they strapped on their weapons and knives. Each ended up also with a handful of grenades, both incendiary and frag.

Brownstone pulled out the small box he'd placed in his

jacket pocket and opened it. It contained two small bottles Shay was certain were magical potions of some sort. Unless the bounty hunter was interested in perfumes in the middle of a fight.

Shay eyed the potions as James slipped them into a pouch on his harness. "For a guy who doesn't like magic, you sure use a lot."

She considered asking him about the amulet. If that wasn't magic, then Peyton had a good sense of fashion. But she also understood Brownstone was entitled to a few secrets, just as she was.

"I *don't* like magic," he explained, "but this is a rescue mission, so I have to be a little more careful. I hope it doesn't come down to using more magic than necessary, but I want to be prepared."

Shay slammed a magazine into her Steyr. "I think I'll just stick to shooting and stabbing people."

Okay, so maybe I'll use the occasional magic knife.

The more jobs she took, maybe the more sense it'd make for her to start stockpiling artifacts for her own personal use. Still, there was something to be said for straightforward weaponry.

Brownstone chuckled as he seated several throwing knives. "Dead is dead. Don't care how." He stood, taking a final moment to check his load-out. "Just so you know, this is about rescuing the woman. I don't need anyone alive to spread rumors about me this time."

See, Professor? Brownstone makes it easy. None of this 'don't kill people' shit.

"Got it. Kill 'em all and let God sort 'em out."

Brownstone grunted. "Let's go say hello to the Harriken."

Shay grunted back, trying to force her voice down an octave. "And goodbye."

The bounty hunter led off with a smile playing on his lips.

Shay trailed after Brownstone as they jogged toward Belmont House, her heart pounding. People talked about how important it was to remain calm in dangerous situations.

She'd always thought that was bullshit.

A little fear got her heart and adrenalin pumping, which translated to her being faster and stronger. The smallest edge in battle could mean the difference between life and death. It could be difficult to ride the line between fight or flight, but for her it was almost *always* worth it.

Ahead of them, a two-story wooden building nestled comfortably among tall pines. From their check on the internet, Belmont House also contained a basement level. They assumed Nicole Anderson was being kept below.

Cars, SUVs, and trucks lined the paved circle drive leading up to the chalet, from luxury models to junkers.

The pair pushed closer to the target.

Over twenty men lingered outside in the circle drive. Half of them appeared to be Harriken, judging by the swords on their sides. The others were a mixed group of non-Japanese men wearing suits, tactical uniforms, or street clothes with obvious gang colors.

It was like a United Nations of scumbags.

Most of the thugs had pistols or submachine guns in their hands. A few carried assault rifles or shotguns. They were ready to play.

Several drones hovered overhead, their rotors lightly whirring, but from a distance, it was hard to tell if they were armed.

"Looks like they know we're here," Shay muttered. "Some drone probably spotted the truck before we pulled off the road. I would have liked a little more surprise. Not a bunch, but at least some."

Brownstone tapped his jammer band. "If they didn't know before, they'll know now. And sometimes it's better for them to know you're coming and be afraid. They'll make more mistakes that way."

"If you say so."

The drones all halted, hovering in place.

One of the suited men yelled something, and the men in the circle drive spread out.

"Remember," Brownstone rumbled. "We don't need survivors. Do what you need to do. Just don't die."

"Good." Shay flipped her Steyr's safety off. "That makes things easier."

"Let's get closer, and you lay down suppressive fire," James ordered. "And I'll close and finish them off."

Shay gave him a mock salute. "Aye, aye, sir! And Brownstone?"

"What?"

"Don't get killed by being stupid. Remember, we're here for a reason."

Brownstone grinned. "I haven't been killed yet, and I do dangerous shit all the time."

Shay rolled her eyes. "It only takes one time, dumbass."

They sprinted through the cover of thick tree trunks in a zigzag pattern. One of the thugs shouted.

Time for the fun.

A fusillade of bullets blasted through the woods. Shay offered a burst in return, taking down a poor gangbanger with a pistol. He'd picked a bad day to make an extra buck.

A quick roll brought Shay behind some douchebag's Lexus. Brownstone kept running. Bullets pelted the car and the tomb raider grinned, satisfied that not only did she have decent cover, but some asshole's car was getting shot up. Even if she died, she'd have her revenge from the grave.

Shay popped up and squeezed off a few quick shots. A Harriken with a rifle dropped to the ground, his neck spewing blood. The thugs began to rush toward the other cars for cover, firing wildly.

Brownstone continuing along the circular drive, following the parked vehicles. Bullet after bullet whizzed by him, throwing up dirt and shattering a windshield here or there.

A thug's submachine gun suddenly flew out of his hand, and Shay blinked. The man hadn't let go. It was as if some invisible force had yanked it from his grip. To the man's credit, he dropped his hand to pull out his pistol without any hesitation.

Shay took the opportunity to fire a burst into his chest, and he fell with a scream. She continued sweeping back and forth until she ran out of bullets. No bastards died, but they also didn't risk anymore shots at Brownstone.

Her failure to continue shooting finally sank in, and the thugs opened up on her. The car window next to her shattered, showering her with safety glass fragments.

"Damn it," Shay muttered. "Should have worn a mask." She shook her head to try to get some of the fragments out of her hair.

Now close to several of the men, Brownstone opened fire, his .45 hurling forth its angry contents. Shay took the opportunity to crouch and swap out her empty magazine.

The remaining thugs had bought a clue by this point, and tried to tighten up their formation while continuing to lay down covering fire.

A bullet ripped into the back of Shay's Lexus shield, and her head jerked up. Three men stood on the balcony, firing down at her and Brownstone.

If those guys were better shots we'd probably be dead. Too damn rusty at this.

The old killer instincts now subsumed the field archaeologist. She raised her gun and held down the Steyr's trigger, pelting the three men with bullets.

Two collapsed where they stood and the third bullet-riddled body fell to the ground, landing with a sickening *thud*. She ejected and replaced the mag.

Brownstone charged from his latest cover position, a bright-red Lamborghini. Four men dropped in the blink of an eye, throwing knives stuck in their throats or hearts. The bounty hunter's .45 delivered quick deaths to several others directly after that.

Their screams overlapped.

Shay fired several bursts off to Brownstone's sides, doing her best to pin the thugs down. The concealed enemies stayed down after one man in desert-pattern camouflage took three bullets in the head for his bravery. He didn't even have time to scream before he died.

The sounds of yelling and footsteps from Shay's opposite side forced her to redirect her attention. Reinforcements from the other side of the chalet had arrived, so she needed to distract them before they flanked both her and the bounty hunter.

Okay, as good as time as any to use one of the toys.

Shay grabbed a frag grenade and pulled the pin. "It's been a while." She grinned as she achieved a beautiful forty-five-degree arc. Three…

"Grenade!" one of the men screamed. Two… They all scattered. One!

Most of the shrapnel pierced two Harriken. They'd have to join the Living Battering Ram from the other night in a mass closed-casket funeral. Two other men groaned, having taken more than a few hits themselves. They might not have been killed outright, but they were on their way to dying.

Huh. I forgot how much fun those things could be.

The other reinforcements hesitated, stunned by the carnage—a rookie mistake.

Shay tossed her other frag grenade toward another group, and her incendiary at the back of a gaudy purple SUV being used for cover by some of the reinforcements. The first explosion wounded only a few men, but the second exceeded her wildest expectations.

The explosion ripped into the SUV's gas tank and a massive fireball erupted from the vehicle, blowing it several feet into the air and setting several men aflame.

The shockwave knocked the nearby attackers to the ground.

The burning men screamed.

Shay took advantage of their confusion and pain to dart toward them and give them a fatal overdose of lead. Hell, some of them she was putting out of their misery. She spun on her heel, blasting the groaning and confused men on the opposite side.

The difference between a thug and a true killer was discipline. Being able to inflict violence was easy—it was human nature—but being able to inflict violence when you were terrified and people were dying around you was a much rarer skill.

Shay waited for more victims, scanning the sides of the chalet and looking up for more balcony snipers. Shots rang out, a mix of Brownstone's .45 and the guards' weapons.

Thirty seconds passed, and no more reinforcements showed up. The enemy must have decided that wasting more lives outside was pointless. Shay spun to check on Brownstone's status. Every other man lay dead or dying, except for one Harriken holding a shotgun.

The wide-eyed man backed up slowly as the bounty hunter stalked toward him. He didn't have his pistol out. Shay waited to see if he intended to stare him to death.

The criminal threw his gun up and squeezed the trigger. "Die, *oni!*" The shotgun jerked as it released its deadly load.

"No!" Shay screamed as Brownstone took a load of buckshot to the chest.

Why did you get so close, you idiot? You should have been smarter.

She blinked. Something wasn't right—or maybe it was more that something wasn't wrong enough.

Brownstone didn't yell or scream. He didn't jerk or fall. He just stood there with a bored looking expression on his face, like he got shot point-blank in the chest every day and it'd lost all meaning or excitement.

The bounty hunter glanced down at his now-shredded shirt and raised a single finger, wagging it back and forth. "You fuckers keep tearing up my clothes. It's really starting to piss me off."

"*Kami-sama tasukete kudasai!*" the Harriken screamed.

Shay had no idea what that meant; maybe a plea for mercy or a prayer to God. It wouldn't matter. Whoever ran the universe from beyond seemed to be favoring James Brownstone that day.

The bounty hunter's expression remained unchanged as he reached out and snatched the shotgun from the man. He cracked the gun over his knee like it was a twig and brained the Harriken with the sharp remains of his own weapon. The man's blood splattered on the bounty hunter.

"And you guys keep staining my shirts, too."

The man collapsed to the ground, and Brownstone wiped some of the blood off his face. He mostly succeeded in spreading it around, making him look even more sinister—like some crazed barbarian from the Dark Ages.

Shay stared, agape. She'd seen people killed in many creative ways in her life, but Brownstone's little display was a first.

"Damn," she muttered.

Brownstone turned to look at her, and she gasped. He stared at her with vertically-slit pupils in speckled yellow and green irises, his eyes more like a cat's than a human's. A few seconds later his normal brown human eyes returned.

Shay couldn't muster up anything to say. The man standing before her went well beyond the bounty hunter who'd raided the Harriken house.

Was he even human?

Shay finally managed to open her mouth to comment when she spotted movement from the balcony out of the corner of her eye. She fired without thought, nailing a Harriken holding a rocket launcher, and before she'd even fully turned the man fell backward, his payload blasting into the balcony's overhang.

A fireball bloomed from the area, its roar deafening. The explosion launched a shower of bodies and wood over the circle drive. The remains of the balcony and the room connected to it burned, smoking pouring into the sky.

"Shit," Shay spat. "We're on the clock now, Brownstone —unless not needing to breathe is also on your lists of skills."

"Nah, still need to do that," Brownstone admitted with a shrug. "Let's go get her."

The bounty hunter reloaded his pistol with a fresh magazine and hurried to the front door. Shay ran after him, sparing a last glance at the shotgunner.

You assholes should never have fucked with him.

22

Ten more men waited inside the building in the foyer. They lasted less than thirty seconds, their screams echoing in the high-vaulted room.

Shay was still off-balance from Brownstone's little trick with the shotgun. The man could be a lot of things, or it might be a side-effect of his magic amulet. She wasn't about to question him about it in the middle of their shared bloodbath.

Brownstone took a moment to survey the bodies. "Huh, no Topknot Guy. I'm kind of disappointed."

If he's some weird creature or Oriceran, he doesn't act like it.

Shay prodded a body with her foot. "Maybe that guy was the local leader, or the head honcho was smart enough to bail when he knew we were coming. Just because the Harriken value strength doesn't mean the guy smart enough to run things is going to stay there and wait for a living tank to show up and kill him."

The bounty hunter grunted. "So I might still have shit to deal with in the future?"

Shay almost wanted to laugh. The Harriken couldn't be stupid enough to come after him again after everything he'd done. That went beyond arrogance to the realm of suicidal stupidity.

"Brownstone, we've killed a lot of people today, and you killed a lot of people the other day. I think the Harriken have gotten the point by now, and if they haven't, well, they don't have anybody left. They'll probably start sending you a fruit basket on your birthday."

The acrid smell of smoke floated from upstairs. "We've got to get moving. I'll take point."

Shay had run out of ammo for her Steyr, so she readied a pistol. *Ah, that gun was so fun, too.*

The smell of smoke grew stronger. The hungry fire would consume Belmont House. From Shay's perspective that also meant it'd do a lot to conceal any evidence of their involvement.

It might be too late to worry about it now, but she preferred not to be the target of another international criminal organization.

Shay rushed after Brownstone down the hallway. They couldn't spend too much time fooling around now that the house was on fire, even if it remained contained to the top floor for the moment.

A minute of searching revealed the basement door, but no other enemies, Harriken or otherwise. They'd finally run out of people to shoot or stab.

Fuck, I was just getting into it, too.

The door wasn't even locked or reinforced, yet more proof of the arrogance of their enemy.

Brownstone nodded to Shay, raising his gun. "Three...two...one!" He threw open the door.

No bullets rang out. The pair rushed down the stairs. The stench of blood hung heavy in the air.

Unlike the storage room at the Harriken house, the Belmont House basement appeared to have once been some sort of torture room. A single table and carts filled with bloodied blades, screws, and pins filled the center of the room. One cart even held a few lead-acid batteries with thick alligator clamps. It was everything a sick-ass psychopath might need.

The elaborate twisted-metal light fixture hanging overhead lacked light bulbs, leaving a dim standing lamp in the corner the only source of light.

Shay twitched, her stomach churning. She might have been a killer, but at least she offered her victims a quick death. Torture was for cowards.

An ebony-skinned woman with long bright-white hair lay on the table, her hands and feet secured by ropes. She wore only a torn dull-green hospital gown. Jagged lacerations, bloodstains, burns, and abrasions covered her body, arms, legs, and face. The fingers on one of her hands were bent at extreme angles. There was some sort of metal sheet around her chest.

Brownstone let out a low growl.

Shay swallowed. She almost wished they could bring the Harriken back to life so they could kill them all again.

"Nicole Anderson?" Brownstone asked, a confused look on his face.

The woman on the table was as dark as night, unlike

her daughter. Despite her white hair, she didn't have a single wrinkle on her face.

Huh. Her daughter can see weird soul shit, and now her mom looks a bit different than we'd expect. So yeah.

Nicole slowly turned her head. "So much screaming. You killed them all, I hope?"

Brownstone grunted. "Yeah, we killed them all. Some of them may take a while to die, though."

"Good. Why? Are you here for what they sought?" Nicole stared at him, her expression weary.

Shay stared at the woman, surprised she wasn't already insane given the obvious level of torture she'd sustained. It was an impressive display of strength of will.

"I'm here because a girl needs her mother." Brownstone pulled out a knife. "I helped your daughter out the other day." He sliced one of the ropes. "Because she helped me with my dog. The Harriken tried to take her, and I made them pay for that. Things escalated from there." He made short work of the other ropes and the metal they had her wrapped in. Magical suppression, maybe? "And so now a lot more Harriken are dead. Things just got...complicated."

Complicated didn't begin to capture the insanity of the situation.

"Is Alison safe?" Nicole weakly pushed herself into a sitting position. "My husband sold me out, and I know he was targeting her too." She sighed and took a deep breath. "I hoped that his twisted mind might at least show some mercy toward his own daughter."

"Alison's safe. We've got her stashed somewhere the Harriken can't find her." Brownstone rubbed his chin. "And I had a discussion with Walt about proper respect for his wife and child. It ended with a broken jaw, and a warning from me that he'd better get the fuck out of town or he would be dead."

Not enough, Brownstone. Not fucking enough. That fucking father needs a little torture himself, or at least a bullet in his head. Selling your own wife out to be tortured?

Nicole nodded slowly, a pleased look on her face. "He loved me once, I think, but still… What he's done is unforgiveable. Please promise me you'll kill him should you get the chance?"

"I gave him my warning. Especially after seeing this shit," he nodded at her. "If I see him again, he's dead."

Shay smiled, glad that everyone was on the same page.

"You have no idea how that quiets my soul." Nicole groaned. Her damaged hand glowed for a second, and the fingers moved back into their proper position. Several of her wounds sealed themselves.

Shay was beginning to think a few things had been kept from Alison.

"I don't get it," she said. "What's worth all this bullshit? Can you see souls like your daughter? Did they want to use you as a lie detector or something?"

Brownstone shrugged. "Does it fucking matter? We can do the Q and A later. This place is on fire, remember? Let's just get her the hell out of here."

Nicole stared at James, not saying a word. He shifted under her gaze, uncomfortable. She coughed some blood into her hand.

"Shit." The bounty hunter reached into his pocket and pulled out the healing potion. "This is magic. It'll help you." He held it out. "Best potions witch in Los Angeles made it."

Nicole wrapped her hand around his and closed his fingers. "Was this potion made for you?"

"Yeah, whatever. You can pay me back later. You're not gonna make it otherwise."

"You don't understand. It won't work. If anything, it'll probably make things worse."

Brownstone winced.

Shay looked between the two. She knew a little about healing potions and knew they couldn't be generic for all types of beings, but one made for humans tended to work on most humans.

Brownstone scrubbed a hand over his face, desperation in his eyes.

"What's your name?" Nicole asked quietly.

"James Brownstone."

She smiled at him, looking him in his eyes. "Thank you, James Brownstone, for all that you have done to aid my daughter. I can die now, secure in the knowledge that she's safe, but there is something you should know."

Shay called over her shoulder, "Like my friend said, the house is on *fire*."

Nicole smiled sadly. "I'll be dead soon anyway. You need to understand what I'm going to tell you."

Brownstone shook his head. "What the fuck is going on?" He looked at Shay before turning back to Nicole.

Shay almost snorted. *It'll be pretty embarrassing if we end up dying from smoke inhalation after killing our way in.*

"My legacy is a *wish*," Nicole said softly. "I ran from my family responsibilities and duties on Oriceran, but it did not change the truth that those in my line are bequeathed a wish."

"A wish?" Shay turned around, surprised. "You mean...like an actual *I wish I were rich* kind of wish?" She didn't even know that kind of magic was real.

Brownstone glanced at Shay, and back at Nicole.

"Something like that. Magic is more powerful and wild than you humans understand." The dark-skinned Drow leaned forward, her long white hair covering her face.

"I wanted to come here and live a simpler life, so I used my magic to disguise myself, took a human husband, and bore a half-human child. But with the truth of Oriceran coming out and my heritage becoming more obvious with the flow of magic each year, my husband figured out the truth. That was fine, since I'd always wanted to tell him anyway, but then I made my true mistake."

"Your true mistake?" Brownstone asked.

Nicole nodded. "I told him everything, including that I had a wish and was saving it for our daughter. Foolish me, I thought he'd understand." She inhaled slowly. "I can give the wish to another, but it has to be done willingly. I refused Walt's request. I knew he would not use it well, but I never suspected he'd partner with such scum to betray me."

She held on to the edge of the table. "They tortured me to try and force me to give them the wish, but I'm two hundred and twelve years old, and I am a princess of an ancient and dangerous line. These maggots could not have broken my will if they'd had another century to do so. I was prepared to die to deny them what they'd steal from my child, despite the pain."

Damn, woman. You're looking great for two hundred and twelve.

Shay had faced ice witches, Russian spirits, and naga, but she still managed to be surprised by magic.

Brownstone stared at the woman, not saying anything. There was confusion and concern in his eyes.

Heavy footfalls sounded from above. Someone else wanted to kill them before the fire had a chance to do the job. They didn't have time to play biography with the Oriceran woman.

"Damn it," Shay hissed. "I'm hearing movement upstairs, Brownstone. We need to move *now*."

Nicole slid off the table and slowly made her way toward the stairs, passing James.

Brownstone grabbed her arm. "What are you doing?" He leaned over. "You stay here. We'll deal with the assholes upstairs, then we'll figure something out. I may not know much about healing and magic and shit, but I solve problems." He jerked a thumb upwards. "These types of problems."

Nicole shook her head and smiled grimly. "It's too late for me. Too much of my magic has been expended trying to save my life."

"Can't we take you to some Oriceran healer to help you?"

She shook her head. "No. To keep myself alive, I've been feeding off my own life force. All things have a cost. At this point I'm only delaying the inevitable, but I have enough magic left for one important task."

"What's that?"

Nicole's expression and eyes hardened. "*Vengeance*."

Shay blinked a few times. The Oriceran woman kept her priorities straight, and Shay could appreciate that.

Brownstone released her arm. "We've killed two housefuls of Harriken already."

"Do you think my vengeance too much, human? I would destroy these men over and over if I had the ability."

"Brownstone killed dozens of people for murdering his dog. Trust me, he's not judging you...and I've got my own past."

Whoever is fucking left has it coming and then some. They should be fed to some naga.

Nicole's eyes glinted in satisfaction. "Then you understand what I must do, and *why* I must do it."

Brownstone nodded. "I just wanted you to know that no matter what happens, they've already felt pain. And I hope they feel more." He glanced at Shay. "We'll back you up. These fuckers would kill us anyway, and I don't mind going after a few more after what I just saw."

Shay nodded in agreement.

Nicole shook her head. "No, I may not be able to fully control myself when I do what I must do. You have killed my enemies and saved my daughter. I'd not wish to kill you by accident."

Shay stepped away from the stairs after Brownstone gave her a reluctant nod. She wasn't about to tell some centuries-old Oriceran how to go about getting her revenge.

Nicole padded toward the stairs, something elegant and lethal in her movements. "These men will learn why you do not earn the wrath of a princess of the Drow."

Brownstone looked at Shay and she shrugged. She didn't know much about what a Drow was, let alone anything about their royalty.

"Do not come up if you value your lives." Nicole went up the stairs, determined.

Shay whistled as the Drow turned the corner above. "You ever wonder what would happen if the Oricerans decided they want to take over?"

Brownstone grunted. "No, they're just like us. Lots of good people. Lots of assholes."

"Man, I feel for her…" Shay shook her head. "Fuck, I am her, except I'm not centuries old and magical."

"What do you mean?"

"I just got tired of my old life, too. Wanted something different."

Brownstone eyed her. "Being a tomb raider isn't simpler."

"Didn't say simpler, just different. But I wonder if I'm doomed the same way."

"What are you talking about? You don't have any wish to steal."

Shay sighed and nodded toward the stairs. "No, I just meant no matter how much I run, maybe my past will always catch up with me."

"Maybe, or you can just keep running." Brownstone shrugged. "And thanks for your help. You didn't have to do any of this."

"Don't worry about it." Shay gestured around the torture chamber. "After seeing this, I only regret that I'm not getting to kill—"

The sound of automatic weapons fire rang out above, along with screams.

"Looks like she's starting the party," Shay muttered.

23

Shay paced at the bottom of the stairs. "I don't hear any more gunfire or screaming." She shook her head. "We should have been up there, not sitting here in the basement of a burning building like some dumbass JV kill squad."

Brownstone shrugged. "When someone gives you a warning like that, you listen."

"And what if they killed her?" Shay didn't want any asshole leaving the property alive.

"She was already dying. You heard it, and if they did, the answer is simple."

Shay put her hands on her hips. "Oh? Enlighten me with your great wisdom then, Brownstone."

"The answer is, we kill the people who killed her."

"Okay, fair enough. I like that plan."

Brownstone grunted. "Anyway, you're right. Whatever happened is over. Let's go."

They pulled their guns and hurried up the stairs. Thick

smoke hugged the ceiling, and the crackle and hiss of the fire grew louder.

Shay coughed as she ran through the room. "Yeah, leaving's definitely a good idea."

The pair traveled down the hallway to where four new bodies lay on the ground.

"Grayson," Brownstone commented as he viewed their patches. "I know these guys. Mercenaries. Real scum. Never really had a run in with them since we hang in different circles, but I've known people who have. They'd shoot their own mothers for money."

Shay despised mercenaries like Grayson. They liked to pretend they were anything but hitmen in fancy uniforms. A criminal should at least be honest about what they are.

"Yeah, I've heard of them." Shay's nose wrinkled as she gestured to the three crispy corpses. "Smells like burnt pork."

The bounty hunter's gaze shifted from the burn victims to the other man, who had a clean hole in his throat. The Drow woman had been tortured for days, and still took out trained mercenaries with ease. If she'd been killed, it hadn't been in this hallway.

The pair rushed toward the front door, both coughing. They paused for a moment to search for live enemies, but seeing only bodies, they stepped outside. It took them a moment to separate the people they'd killed from the mercenaries Nicole had destroyed.

"I pity the cops who have to investigate this shit," Brownstone remarked.

Shay was liking what she was seeing. Fire and weird magic. No one would ever link any of this shit to her.

The real assholes got what was coming, and she'd get away.

She shrugged. "They'll play it off as some sort of gang war gone bad, or maybe even a gang summit gone bad. When it's scumbags killing scumbags, it's not like the cops try that hard. I think they think that every dead gangster means the world's a safer place."

"What the fuck?" Brownstone said, looking at half a body. He shook his head. "Can't say I've seen that before."

Shay leaned down and poked her gun through a hole in a dead mercenary. "If this is what she does when she's weak, I'd hate to see what she's like when she's at the top of her game."

Those Harriken bastards got real lucky to find whatever they used to knock out her magic. Otherwise, she would have made Brownstone's shit look like kindergarten.

Both turned at the sound of a soft moan. They rushed to the source and found Nicole kneeling on the ground, blood covering the front of her hospital gown.

Shay shook her head, awed by the level of destruction the Drow on death's door visited upon the mercenaries. If a woman was going to go out, taking dozens of bastards with her was an epic way to do it.

"You okay?" Brownstone asked, reaching down.

Nicole put out a hand and let him help her stand as she stared at the burning Belmont House. The fire had engulfed the entire structure now, the conflagration sending a thick plume of smoke into the sky.

Part of the roof collapsed with a loud groan.

"Glad we're not in there anymore," Shay muttered. "Be pretty weak to die in a fire after going through all that."

Nicole smiled at Brownstone and spoke softly. "I wish I'd married a man like you."

Brownstone grunted. "Trust me, you wouldn't wish that if you knew me that well. I don't think I'm marriage material for you or anyone else on this planet or Oriceran."

"I know that my daughter's own father was prepared to sell her to criminals for power, and you, a man who didn't even know her, *protected* her."

Shay thought that over and nodded to herself. Nicole was right. Brownstone tried to act like he didn't give a shit about anything but bounty money, but everything he'd done was straight-up heroic.

Even her jaded heart threatened to open.

Shit. So much for keeping my distance.

Brownstone shook his head. "I'm paying my debts. She helped me find my dog when he was missing. There's nothing more here. I pay my debts so I don't owe anyone. I like my life simple."

Keep telling yourself that, Brownstone, and you might eventually believe it.

"You told me about all the men you've killed." Nicole waved a hand around, "You're trying to tell me this is just about paying a debt concerning your dog?"

He looked at the carnage around them and turned back to her, running a hand through his hair. "Like I said, things got complicated. I was trying to simplify them."

Nicole weakly laughed. "Most men do everything they can to declare their honor and glory to the world. Are you so afraid of admitting you're a good man, James Brownstone?"

Shay chuckled under her breath.

Brownstone snorted. "I killed a lot of people this week. 'Good man' would be stretching it. Some might say I'm okay or useful, but I don't think anyone would say I'm a *good* man."

"James, I've lived on Earth for decades, and I still find human morality strange. You worry over the strangest things, while letting the meaningless and trivial things distract you."

"Probably shouldn't have moved to L.A. if you wanted a place with people who aren't easily distracted by meaningless trivia."

Brownstone shot her a harsh look.

She shrugged, putting up her hands. "Just sayin'."

Nicole sighed. "It's taking all my control to keep my power from consuming the last of me, but I will die satisfied, knowing that at least I saved you from these fake soldiers."

Brownstone glanced at the dead mercenary company commander. Grayson had access to some heavy weaponry, and unlike the Harriken, they had hardcore battlefield experience. He wasn't so sure he could have escaped unscathed from an encounter with them, let alone brought Shay through.

"We can still take you somewhere," he whispered. "It doesn't have to end this way."

She shook her head. "No, it ended the second Walt betrayed me. There's nothing anyone could do, even back on Oriceran." Nicole wrapped her arms around herself and took a shuddering breath. "I need you to take care of my daughter, the new Princess of the Shadow Forged. I've harmed her by keeping her heritage from her, and I just hope she'll forgive me."

"I… shit." Brownstone rubbed the back of his neck. "All she wants is for you to come back."

Tears ran down Nicole's face as she shook her head. "I know, but there's nothing I can do. My time is done, and I must see to her future. And that's why *I need you.*"

Shay sighed and looked away. It was a terrible way to go out, and she couldn't begin to imagine the pain of dying knowing she was leaving a daughter behind.

Brownstone sighed. "I'll make sure she's taken care of," he finally said. "You have my word."

"Oh, I know that she'll be taken care of, James Brownstone. I can see it in you."

"Is there anything we can do? I could call a priest to give you last rites. I don't know if it works over the phone, but it's something. Or is there someone else we can call?"

"It's okay. My ways are different, even if ultimately it all goes back to the same source."

Brownstone's face hardened with frustration. He needed to learn this lesson, that no matter how powerful he was, there were some problems he couldn't solve.

Shay said nothing. As a woman still adjusting to the idea of even having real friends and helping them out, she didn't know what to say.

The Drow princess placed a gentle hand on the bounty hunter's shoulder. "I can see that this worries you, but don't blame yourself. You've punished the people who have done this to me, and you saved my daughter. That's all I could ask or hope for in this horrible situation."

Brownstone averted his gaze, no quips coming to his mind for once.

Nicole looked at Shay with a sly smile. "I see so much now that I'm using my full abilities once more."

Shay frowned. "Like?" She didn't like the sound of that at all.

She smirked. "Even now your heart is choosing, and there isn't a damn thing you're going to be able to do about it when it is finished."

Fuck, like mother like daughter, huh? I've got to say something. Brownstone will get the wrong idea. Just because I helped him raid a gangster hideout and kill dozens of people and think he's pretty badass doesn't mean much of anything. Not really. Not even because of his abs.

Shay narrowed her eyes. "Not to be rude, but what the hell are you talking about?"

Brownstone shot Shay another glare.

Stay out of this, Brownstone. This is a chick thing.

Nicole stepped toward him, though she kept her focus on Shay. "I'm going to make it easier for you to choose." A mischievous smile appeared on her face.

The Drow threw her arms around his neck and stuck her tongue down his throat.

Shay blinked hard several times. This time she couldn't deny the fire flaring inside of her. It was pure jealousy. It didn't help that Brownstone didn't push the dying woman off right away.

Fuck you. Is it that I'm not old enough? Oh, Shay, you're only twenty-seven, and I only date chicks over two hundred.

Shay loudly cleared her throat in irritation.

Nicole's hold on him slackened, and she collapsed.

Brownstone grabbed her before she hit the ground and she shuddered, her eyes unfocused. A seizure wracked her.

Shay's irritation collapsed under her concern. A woman was about to die in front of her, and she didn't have it coming.

"Come closer," Nicole said quietly. "I have something to tell you."

Brownstone lowered his head near her mouth. "What? Is there anything I can do?"

Nicole whispered something to him.

His eyes narrowed. "What the hell?"

She continued whispering, touching him gently on the chest.

Brownstone furrowed his brow. "You don't know me. I'm a bad man. The only thing that has ever truly loved me was a dog, and I couldn't even keep him from getting killed by the Harriken. I'm a monster, and the only reason I'm tolerated is because people need me to fight bigger monsters. You can't trust me, and you *shouldn't* trust me."

She weakly patted him on the chest and continued whispering.

Nicole coughed up blood and said something else Shay couldn't make out.

"You can't…"

Brownstone stopped as a black mist began to rise from Nicole's body, as it slowly grew lighter and less substantial as the mist continued to rise. He held onto her until there was nothing left of the woman except a torn and bloody hospital gown.

The black mist slowly floated into the sky. From afar a

person could easily mistake it for the plume of smoke from the burning house.

It was over. Shay could ask Brownstone what Nicole had said… later.

Shay walked over and touched his arm. "Brownstone let's get the fuck out of here. We've done what we can, and at least everyone involved has been punished. Sometimes vengeance is all you can achieve."

He nodded slowly, still staring after the black mist as it rose to the heavens.

24

S hay glanced at Brownstone as she drove to her place. They'd stopped over at Alison's house to take care of her father. She'd not been so satisfied with a kill in a while.

Brownstone had been quiet after that other than explaining that the kiss was about transferring the wish to him. He was now the custodian of the legacy of a Drow princess. So much for his simple life.

He then drove to church before they headed back to get her car and head to her place. Shay almost snorted at the thought.

She wasn't sure what she believed about God. In a world with so much magic, it was hard to deny anymore there could be a supernatural creator of everything. She also doubted he'd have an issue with Walt Anderson checking out early to chill with the man downstairs or reincarnate as a dung beetle.

Shay didn't know what the priest told Brownstone

inside the church, but she didn't like the brooding regret on the bounty hunter's face.

She glanced over at him. "I don't know what crawled up your super-armored butt, but shit happens, you know, Brownstone. You have to shake it off. This can't be the first time something's gone south for you."

"My life went south from the beginning."

"I mean, look, we both have our issues, but you did the right thing back there, and you're doing the right thing with the girl. And you got revenge for both the Anderson women."

"I wasn't supposed to get revenge. I was supposed to bring Nicole back to her daughter."

Regret. Shay understood that far too well, but she also understood the way it could grow and strangle you until nothing but the regret remained.

Shay shook her head. "We were both supposed to bring her back, but we didn't make it in time. That's the cold reality. You got some time magic in your warehouse, Brownstone? Otherwise it doesn't matter, and beating yourself up over it isn't going to help." She sighed. "You know the real difference between men and women?"

"Dicks and pussies?"

That elicited a snort from Shay. *At least the man's sense of humor was intact.* "That too. No. It's that women understand, like on the level of our DNA, that not everything can be fixed, that sometimes you just have to roll with it, but men, oh you men, somewhere you're always thinking, I can fix this shit. Just give me a big enough tool."

Shay fought down a wince and hoped Brownstone didn't follow-up on the obvious dirty joke set-up.

Instead, he chuckled. "Maybe. Things are still weird."

"Given some of the shit I've seen you do, I'm surprised to hear that. Weird is really kind of relative, you know?"

He shrugged. "Kicking ass, I get. Bringing in the bad guys, I get. Taking care of a girl? Some girl who's half-Oriceran. What if I fuck her up?"

"Can't do worse than the dad who tried to sell her to a group of gangsters who were torturing her mom."

Brownstone winced. "Yeah, suppose so."

"Don't overthink it, Brownstone. Kicking ass is more your strength." Shay grinned and winked. She couldn't believe the man was so down on himself after all the sweet, sweet vengeance he'd delivered.

This may mean I'm more fucked up than Alison thinks. Just because she can see my soul doesn't mean she's right about everything.

The Spider pulled up to her nice two-story brownstone townhouse with an attached garage. She'd made sure not to move in next to any stash houses this time.

"Nice place," Brownstone muttered.

Shay smirked. "Hey, Brownstone, how do you like my brownstone?"

"You've been probably waiting to say that for days." He snorted. "You should quit trying to be a tomb raider and take up stand-up comedy. I'm sure there's some magic that can actually make you funny."

"You know I'm as funny as I am hot." Shay pressed a button on a garage door opener connected to her sun visor then parked the car. A sober look settled over her face. "I'll let you take the lead on whatever you want to tell Alison."

Brownstone's only response was a nod as they got out of her Spider.

Shay tapped a code into a pad near the door and moved her head forward for a retinal scan. The door clicked open.

"Actual security, see? On the house, not just the Red Room of Pain."

He followed her inside. Two earth-toned love seats dominated the living room, a huge TV hung on the back wall. Fine white carpet covered most of the floor. A quartz-topped island lay in the center of her kitchen. The overall vibe on his first impression was clean and modern, yet comfortable.

Shay loved the new place and her sense of style, but her stomach tightened at the thought of Captain Tight Butt doing a dust test with his finger.

"Whatever you do, don't look in my refrigerator or my cabinets."

"Why? You got body parts in there?"

"Nope. Because it's not all fancy and organized. Your OCD will explode."

"I'm not OCD. I just like to keep things…"

"Simple." Shay finished his sentence for him, giving a short laugh. "Sure, and let's not even get into my bedroom." A few beats passed, and she added in a sultry voice, "Unless you ask nicely."

Brownstone plopped himself down on a love seat and didn't say anything in response.

The lack of even a playful response hurt, but she didn't dare show it on her face. She was still half-convinced Brownstone was gay, *and yet* still interested in him as something more than a slaughter partner. Go figure.

"You're so boring," Shay muttered.

"Better boring than annoying."

"You're that, too."

Light footfalls sounded from the stairs, and Alison made her way down, tightly gripping the bannister. The girl stopped at the bottom on the stairs and looked at Brownstone, her eyes as unfocused as always.

"What?" Brownstone asked.

A huge smile spread across her face. "You're glowing brighter. It's so beautiful. I wish you could see it."

Shay managed not to sigh and looked away.

"I... I'm gonna be straight with you, kid." Brownstone waited for Alison to come join them.

"Nothing good follows a sentence like that."

"We found the place where your mom was, and we, uh..."

"I listen to the news, Mr. Brownstone. I know you just think I'm a kid, but I'm not an idiot. I heard about what happened. It's kind of a big deal, even on national news. They are calling it World War G."

"World War G?"

"World War Gangster."

Shay nodded, satisfied. At least her theory about what the cops would think was correct. That took a little pressure and punishment off her good deed. If one could count facilitating bloody vengeance a good deed.

Brownstone rubbed the back of his neck. "A lot of that... violence happened going in. We found your mom, but she was already in bad shape by the time we rescued her."

Shay watched him for a moment, giving him time to

decide about disclosing the torture. The girl didn't need to know in her opinion. The people responsible were already dead.

Alison's lip quivered, and she gave a curt nod. "She's dead, right?" She swallowed hard.

"Yes. I'm sorry."

The girl sighed. "I almost kind of knew. But I don't understand why all of this happened."

Brownstone took a moment to gather his thoughts.

"You're special, and she was special. More than you realize. Your mom wasn't from around… here."

"A lot of people aren't from California."

Yeah, tell me about it, kid.

Brownstone managed a chuckle. "Your mom was two hundred and twelve years old, Alison. She was Oriceran, some sort of Drow Princess."

"What's a Drow Princess?"

Shay and the man exchanged glances before he continued. "We're not totally sure on that, and we'll have to ask around, discreetly. It's something we're gonna keep to ourselves for now, so no one else comes after you."

Alison moved over to a love seat. "That explains a lot of stuff. Like why I can see what I can see and my hair."

"Your hair? Did it change?"

Shay looked at the girl's hair. It looked the same to her, black with frosted tips.

"I don't dye my hair, Mr. Brownstone, and I know there are white parts. It didn't used to be like this. Dad told me to dye it all black when it started happening, but Mom wouldn't let him. Now I get why. It must be some Drow thing."

"You'll probably get darker as you age, your skin. And, yeah, your hair will get lighter. Your mom had incredible magic, so maybe you'll get that, too. I don't know."

Alison bit her lip and nodded. "What happens from here? I can't go back with my dad even if he wanted me."

Yeah, we made that kind of impossible anyway.

Brownstone let out a breath he didn't even realize he'd been holding. "I'm gonna take care of you. At least for now."

The girl looked down, her breathing shallow. Shay didn't feel much pain when she left her parents. She hated them both, but at least this girl had grown up for some years in a happy family.

This is the price of love and friendship.

Shay wasn't so sure if it was worth it, but she also wasn't sure if it wasn't. She sighed and headed toward the kitchen.

"You don't have to stay with me if you don't want to," Brownstone said. "I'm not good with kids. If you have some other relatives, I can help track them down. I'm not good with anyone, really, but I have space, and I'm clean."

"Very fastidious," she muttered from the kitchen as she filled a glass of water.

"I don't have any relatives that I know of." Alison smiled. "I wish to stay with you."

"Okay, kid, your funeral."

Shay watched the two, a soft smile on her face. After all the pain and suffering, at least the girl would have some hope for the future.

Alison laughed and looked over at Shay. "Is she gonna be my new mom?"

Shay choked on her glass of water, spewing droplets onto her countertop. "What? No, no, no. I'm not old enough to be a mom. Uh. I'll be the *aunt*." She nodded, a satisfied look on her face. "Yeah, that sounds perfect. I'm the aunt. Or the hot older sister."

"I like aunt better."

Brownstone shrugged. "That's more than what I was going to ask. At least now when I ask you to babysit, it'll be your niece, so you can't bitch too much."

Alison frowned and shook her finger at him. "I don't need a babysitter. I'm a teenager, not a little girl."

Shay grinned. Brownstone thought fighting the Harriken was tough, now he had to deal with the real threat, a teenager.

"Whatever. We'll figure it out later." Brownstone shrugged. His phone buzzed, and he pulled it out. "Oh, I almost missed it. Hey, do you mind if I watch some *Barbeque Wars?* With all this fun lately, I don't even know what's happening on my favorite show."

Always the priorities. Huh, Brownstone? "Be my guest. The voice recognition's on for the TV."

"Don't you have a remote? I fuc…" Brownstone glanced over at Alison and caught himself. "I don't like voice recognition systems. They always have trouble with my voice. It's like they think I'm background noise or something."

Shay rolled her eyes. "You do have the weirdest problems, Brownstone."

After thirty minutes of listening to Brownstone explain the finer points of sauce ingredient counterpoints and the advantages of different cooking temperatures, Alison excused herself and headed up to the guest room, a faint smile on her face.

Shay watched as the girl walked up the stairs. The minute her back was turned, Shay's smile disappeared. "I've got to go check on something. I'll be back in a few minutes."

"Sure, okay." Brownstone barely nodded. He was too engrossed in one of the judge's acerbic takedowns of the perceived failure of a contestant's experimental "Divine Sauce."

"There's only one real God Sauce. And that's at Jessie Rae's. Fool shouldn't have stepped up if he couldn't really bring it."

Shay resisted a scoff and hurried up the stairs until she stood in front of the guest room door. She knocked lightly.

"Come in," Alison said.

Shay opened the door and found Alison hugging the pillow on the bed, her eyes tear-streaked.

"Thought so." Shay quietly came in and shut the door behind her. "You don't have to hide away if you want to cry about your mother, Alison."

The girl shook her head. "I didn't want Mr. Brownstone to see me like this. It'll make him feel bad, and he's already done so much."

Shay sat down on the edge of the bed next to her "He may only have two settings when it comes to showing emotion. There's asshole or clueless. But that doesn't mean he expects you to be like that, too."

"You don't understand, Shay." Alison sniffled. "That's not what I'm worried about."

"Explain it to me. I know about pain, Alison. I can't say I've always dealt with pain well, but I do know what it can do to your heart and mind."

"I don't want to cry and make him feel worse, though." The teen sucked in a deep breath. "I can tell by the way he's talking and his energy that he blames himself. He thinks he let me down or something. I wanted my mom back, but it's not Mr. Brownstone's fault. It's my dad's fault and those Harriken guys. I was happy when I heard about them being killed on the news."

Shay stared at Alison, taken aback by the girl's insight. They would have to stop underestimating her.

"You don't worry about Brownstone. You worry about yourself. He's the adult… well, adultish person, and you're the teenager. No one's gonna blame you for being sad over your mom dying. It's what we'd expect."

Alison nodded. Her face twitched as she threw her arms around Shay and the girl's restraint shattered. She sobbed into the woman's chest.

"Mom…"

They sat there on the bed like that for several minutes, Shay stroking Alison's hair while the girl cried out a tsunami of tears over all that she'd lost. The tsunami became a mere wave, then finally a shallow trickle.

"Sorry," Alison sniffled out, her cheeks and eyes red. "I… I told myself that I wasn't gonna do this. I told myself I was gonna be strong."

Shay pulled away and smiled. "Leave the stone-faced attitude for Brownstone. You'll have years to learn to bottle up all your emotions in a screwed-up way like the rest of us. For now, revel in the fact you're still allowed to feel."

The sadness vanished on Alison's face, replaced by fiery anger.

Shay blinked, wondering if she'd said something to piss the girl off. Normally, she didn't care, but kicking a grieving kid while she was down wasn't her style.

"I wish he wouldn't have let him go." Alison sat up straighter.

"What are you talking about?"

"Mr. Brownstone. He let my dad go. He'll come back for me."

Shay gave a satisfied smile. "Don't worry about your dad. James made *sure* that your dad would never come after you again."

Alison looked up, a question on her face, but none emerged from her mouth. The girl exhaled softly and nodded.

Be glad you're not asking, kid. Sometimes it's better not to know for sure.

25

Shay frowned as she rolled up to Alison's former home. A rusty van sat parked in the driveway, and the front door was open.

Alison was still at Brownstone's place and would stay there for a while. The bounty hunter had tracked down a magic school that she could attend, but for the moment, she would relax with her foster father. He still needed to research the school and make sure it was safe for the girl.

Someone was there who shouldn't be inside. Shay sighed. She'd come over to look through a few things and help the girl get an idea on what she might want to keep.

Seriously? Looting their house already? What a shitty neighborhood.

Shay threw open her car door and marched up to the house. No one was in the living room. She stepped inside and leaned against the wall. Someone was chatting with someone else in a nearby bedroom. Shay continued to wait.

Two skinny punks stepped out of the bedroom, both

with pillow cases. The pillow cases were misshapen and straining with the items they'd already collected.

Shay laughed. "You're robbing my niece's place, and you're using pillow cases? Pathetic. I'm fucking insulted."

The men dropped their loot and both pulled out knives.

"Better run now, bitch, if you know what's good for you." The wiry kid snarled at her, curling his lip to show a gold crown.

Shay shook her head. "I've had an annoying time of it lately. A friend of mine had to go through stuff, cobra tried to eat me, you know the usual."

The men blinked and exchanged glances.

Shay whipped her gun out in one fluid motion. "I'd appreciate it if you didn't try and piss me off even more, assholes."

The men dropped their knives and lifted their hands. "Hey, hey, hey. Chill. We were just messing around, you know?"

Shay stepped away from the front door and motioned toward it with her free hand. "Get the fuck out. If you come back, I'll shoot you in the balls and let you suffer for five minutes before I shoot you in the head. Do you understand me?"

"Yeah, yeah. Yes, ma'am."

The men sprinted for the door, their faces ashen.

Shay slammed the door shut with her boot and holstered her weapon. "Time to look around."

Shay had developed an eye for unusual hiding spots. She was a tomb raider and a paranoid ex-killer who liked to hide things from her enemies. She found the electronic wall safe hidden behind a false panel in the master bedroom closet in no time.

Shay tapped Alison's birthday into the numeric keypad. The safe clicked open. Nicole might have been a centuries-old magical princess and living WMD, but she wasn't all that different from many other parents.

Several small items sat inside the case. There was a multi-colored shell, a large tooth, a bone ocarina, among others. Every tomb raider instinct in Shay screamed they were magical artifacts.

"Looks like I have a little research to do for Alison."

Shay returned to her car to pull out a box from the passenger seat. She headed back into the bedroom to load up the artifacts. It was time for a little trip to Warehouse Five.

Her phone rang.

"What, Peyton? I told you I'd be busy for a few hours."

"Yeah, yeah. Look, just come to your… third place as soon as you can. A time-sensitive job opportunity came up. Like you need to leave tonight time-sensitive."

Shay sighed. "Okay, fine. I have to go do something first. I'll be there in about an hour and a half."

Shay secured all the doors. She wasn't sure if the looters would come back, but after her display with her gun, they'd stay away at least for a couple of days.

Probably nothing here as important as the artifacts.

Shay's gaze froze on a picture of Nicole hugging Alison. Her skin tone was lighter and her hair darker. The picture didn't look that old, maybe a couple of years. She tossed it in the box.

No, there's a lot of stuff here as important as the artifact. Don't worry, Alison. I'll help you get what you need.

Shay sipped her beer as Brownstone sat across from her gobbling down ribs. She liked barbecue well enough, and it'd be a long while before she would prefer the food over pizza, but she'd figured the bounty hunter would be more comfortable this way.

She patted the box next to her. She'd not dare leave it in her car. Replacing a sports car was easy. Artifacts not so much, but she planned to stop off at Warehouse Five after talking with Peyton.

"She's adjusting better than I thought she would." Brownstone gnawed on a bone. "Considering everything that's happened."

"Well, she can see souls. She knows there's people who give a shit about her and are willing to take care of her."

"Yeah. You think I'm doing the right thing with this School of Necessary Magic?"

Shay shrugged. "What the fuck do I know about raising kids? I'll tell you this, that girl needs guidance. I'll check through my sources on this place to make sure it's okay, though. That help?"

Brownstone grunted. "Yeah. It does."

"I've got a job coming up. I'll be out of town for a day or two. Just so you know."

The experience of worrying about Brownstone knowing her business was odd. Peyton had been the only person in a long time that she bothered to inform of anything. She couldn't escape the truth that she had a new friend. A friend that she wanted to be something more.

How the fuck did I end up with some magic-using bounty hunter as a friend?

His gaze lifted from his ribs. "Did you need backup for the job?"

Shay was tempted. Sorely tempted, but right now, Alison needed stability.

"I'm good." Peyton would not have picked a job that required her to bring help. "But thanks for the offer."

Brownstone picked up his beer and took a sip. "I'm sure I can always find a bounty in the area if you need me along. I know you didn't have to help me with the Harriken."

"No, I didn't. But don't think you don't owe me. I'll make you come along when I need you." Shay grinned and winked. "For now, just live in fear."

The man laughed quietly, no tension on his face.

"Try and not start any gang wars when I'm gone, Brownstone."

He shrugged. "No promises."

Two suitcases lay packed on tables near the southern walls of Warehouse Three when Shay arrived. Peyton stood over an open suitcase, counting 9mm magazines wearing jeans and a jean jacket.

"Okay, I'm here." Shay stifled a yawn. "What's with the jean tuxedo and what's the big hurry?"

"A million-dollar job. But you don't even have to recover anything. And this is retro bougie."

Shay moved over to unzip a suitcase. She wanted to double-check the loadout. "What do you mean?"

"This isn't a recovery job. It's a... stop the recovery job."

Shay sorted through some of the devices packed. Good assortment of jammers and some drones. "I'm not taking hit contracts, Peyton." She frowned. "I'm surprised you'd even suggest it."

He waved his hands in front of him. "It's not like that. It's simple. No killing. The client wants you to travel to Ohio. There's a recently discovered cavern right next to the Great Serpent Mound, an over 1300-foot effigy mound built by the Native American Fort Ancient culture."

"I know about it. That thing has been studied for a long time, over a century. How the fuck did they miss a cave all this time?"

"That's just it. They are pretty sure it *wasn't* there until recently. Some sort of magical spell wearing off is the theory."

Shay nodded. "Got it. What's in the cave?"

"Archaeologists recovered an artifact inside recently, as in yesterday. They've not publicized it yet, and they don't want to move it until they understand it better, because they've done some tests and know it's magic. They've not even mentioned discovering the cave to the general public. The whole area has been sealed off."

Shay zipped up the suitcase. "Our boy wants me to grab this artifact then? I don't get it. How is that different than any other job?"

"Nope. He wants you to destroy it."

"Huh? Why?"

"He won't say."

Shay frowned. "He won't say?"

Peyton shook his head. "No, but he will pay a million for confirmed destruction of the artifact. All you need to do is smash it up and grab a handful of the pieces as proof of the artifact. He'll pay out based on that."

"I've never heard of a person who wants to pay to destroy an artifact. Fuck, just think of how much you can make to sell it. Something smells off."

"I thought so too, and I checked into it." Peyton pulled his phone out of his pocket. A few taps and swipes later he held it up. A picture of a tall humanoid skeleton with double rows of teeth, elongated jaw, and long claws was on the screen. "This skeleton is eight feet tall."

"Oh, yeah, I've heard about this sort of thing. People claim that they've found all sorts of weird skeletons all over the country. I figure most of them are just some unlucky Oriceran bastards who got stuck on old Earth."

"This was found in the same chamber as the artifact." Peyton swiped again and revealed a picture of a worn clay bowl covered with glyphs. "This is the artifact."

Shay peered at the image. "What about these glyphs?"

Peyton grinned. "That's where things get interesting. They resemble ancient Akkadian cuneiform."

"As in ancient Mesopotamia? That's a long way and time from the Native culture that built the mound."

"Yep. Really old version too, we're talking pre-third millennium BC."

Shay rubbed her chin. "Talk about your out-of-place artifact. Do you have any sort of translation? I don't give a shit how rough."

"A lot of the writing isn't legible off the pictures, and

I've not been able to track down any X-ray or other frequency scans, but the little I've found isn't good. Um, well, there's a lot of holes in it, and I'm not an expert in ancient Akkadian. I used a progr—"

"Spit it out," Shay snapped.

Peyton swiped a few times on his phone. "Darkness swallows. Tiamat. New souls. New flesh." He shrugged. "That's all I got, and there are lots of words missing between each of those phrases."

Tiamat. Shay didn't need to be an expert on ancient Akkadian to worry about what the combination of a chaos goddess and an artifact might bring.

"They've found a lot of weird skeletons through the decades like that one," Shay said. "They've always tried to explain it away or cover it up, but last time I checked there was a good 1000 cases that seemed legit, especially if you take Oriceran into account. I wonder if this has something to do with the client."

Peyton nodded slowly. "Yeah, the client's trying to hide his identity, but he's bad news, Shay. Major ties to dark magic underworld. I've been able to sniff out that much."

"In other words, even the assholes don't want this thing in circulation."

Peyton shrugged. "It looks like it's some sort of power play, and we're helping him out."

"Well, it's not gonna hurt the world to remove a little dark magic." Shay grinned. "I'm thinking that I can make a million dollars blowing up some demon-summoning bullshit."

See, Brownstone. I can make money and be a good girl, too.

S hay guided the drone with the virtual thumb stick on her phone as she looked through a night-vision display being fed into her AR goggles.

"This is almost too easy," Shay muttered to herself.

No one was even guarding the cave entrance. They had a few cameras set up, but they wouldn't last a minute against her once she closed on them. The lame gates they'd set up along the approaching roads were easy enough to drive around, and she'd not spotted any cops.

It was like they were depending on their pathetic closure announcement to keep people away. Security by obscurity meant no security at all.

Her feed died.

LOST CONNECTION TO DRONE ALPHA FOUR.

Shay narrowed her eyes. She flipped up her goggles and tapped away at the control app. She couldn't ping the drone at all, but her phone signal was still as strong, which meant no jamming. Someone had taken her drone out.

She sighed. "Okay, so it won't be too easy."

Shay flipped her AR goggles back down and activated the night-vision mode as she stepped out of the rental Chevy truck. She'd flown the drone all the way around and then approached the cave from the opposite side to not draw attention to her vehicle's location.

Shay checked her knives and gun then stepped out of the truck. She didn't have to win some epic fight. She didn't even need to recover the artifact. All she needed to do was smash the thing.

Better not tell Brownstone I'm in a Chevy instead of a Ford.

Shay made her way through a dense patch of trees on one side of the mound. She picked up the occasional owl or fox through her goggles, but nothing remotely human. It was only a small comfort.

They were out there and watching. They had no reason to destroy her drone otherwise.

Shay stayed in the forest rather than hitting the small path running along the mound. At night, it wasn't much of a sight, though she could make out the outline of the raised ground. The recently uncovered cave was about another 200 yards away, near the center of the mound where it twisted up in a near-U pattern

She continued to sweep for any sign of other people but saw nothing. A cracking branch sounded behind her, only a few yards away.

Shay spun her gun at the ready but saw no one. She stared into the night, the eerie green glow of the night vision coloring even the most banal of objects and making them seem otherworldly.

There were no more noises. Shay turned around slowly.

Her free hand moved to her goggles and she tapped a button to switch to infrared mode. She spun back around.

Gotcha, assholes.

Four human IR signatures lit up her display like Christmas lights. They had masculine outlines, she thought.

Shay smirked. "If you don't want to end up dead, put your hands up and shut off whatever bullshit you're using to hide yourself."

The four invisible men walked toward her. Four shots rang out from Shay's gun. The men jerked and fell to the ground. She followed up with four more shots into the downed men. The men didn't move.

Shay switched back to night-vision mode, but the men remained invisible. A quick check back in IR revealed their heat signatures were still there. She didn't know how long it took a dead body to cool down.

The minutes stretched on as she moved forward a few yards at a time, sweeping the area in both night-vision and IR mode. She spotted no other invisible men, but her neck remained stiff.

Fucking assholes have to hide like that.

Her checks on the bodies also confirmed they hadn't gotten back up. Shay's recent experiences had taught her that just because something went down didn't mean it'd stay down.

She approached the cave entrance. She pulled back her sleeve to tap on her wide-frequency jammer. She then put bullets into the cameras set up around the entrance. After a reload, she hurried toward the cave.

Shay switched to normal vision mode and switched on a headlamp as she stepped into the narrow tunnel.

The tunnel widened into a long but short cave containing several small flags marking the corners of string squares. There were no signs the archaeologists had excavated any of the marked areas yet.

The skeleton from the picture, in all its double-jawed, long-taloned glory, lay in the corner, in the center of one of the string squares. A smooth-topped earthen mound held the bowl.

Shay let out a long sigh. Even if the bowl was some sort of evil chaos-demon summoning artifact, the idea of destroying history made her stomach churn.

Curiosity shouldn't put the world at risk.

She lifted her hand to switch back to IR mode and gasped.

In IR, the skeleton glowed as brightly as any of the men she'd killed outside. A half-dozen other large humanoid forms rested against the back of the cave, packed together and leaning against the wall.

Shay frowned, wondering why the archaeologists didn't feel anything even if they hadn't run an IR sweep through the cave. She switched back to normal visual mode and made her way toward where she'd spotted the heat signatures. She holstered her gun and pulled out a knife to tap at the air.

Her knife met something hard. Bone. She was sure of it, even if it wasn't visible to the naked eye.

She looked over her shoulder toward the cave entrance. Even if IR mode wouldn't help her make out many details, the men she'd shot outside looked about normal height.

She didn't understand the link between the invisible giants and the normal-sized men.

Shay returned to normal visual mode and made her way back over to the bowl. She set her phone on the ground at an angle to record and made sure to light up the artifact with her lamp. Her right hand lifted, gun in hand.

A few deep breaths followed, and she pulled the trigger. The bowl shattered. Shards blasted in every direction.

"Whoa... That was easy."

A magical clay bowl is about as strong as any other clay bowl.

She grabbed several handfuls of the shards from different places on the ground and slipped them into her pouch. The client mentioned separating them from the main bowl, but he seemed to be more concerned with the basic destruction of the artifact.

It wouldn't hurt to store a few of the fragments in Warehouse Five given she'd already shattered the bowl.

Shay made her way into the cave entrance and pulled out a couple of grenades. Her stomach tightened, and she made a mental note to consider avoiding any job that required her to destroy historical evidence.

Shay pulled the pin and tossed the grenades inside. She was clear of the entrance when it exploded.

Thick smoke poured from the cave as Shay surveyed the area. She spotted no one with her light and normal vision nor with night vision.

I better check to make sure those guys are still dead.

A tap switched her to IR mode. Her heart kicked into a gallop. The four men she'd shot before still lay exactly where she left, but dozens of heat signatures were making their way through the woods toward the cave. Several of them towered over the others, their bodies too broad and their limbs too long to be human.

Guttural growls filled the air.

Fuck. Yeah, bet you have talons and two rows of teeth, huh?

The humans, at least she assumed they were humans based on size, moved toward her. Their strides were even and long, but they didn't run.

Shay sprinted toward the woods. She opened up with her gun and emptied her clip into the charging men. Fourteen men dropped to the ground, and she reloaded. Her arrival in the trees forced her back into the night-vision mode.

Low-hanging branches slapped at the charging tomb raider. Her lungs burned as she continued her charge back toward her rental truck. The growls grew louder and closer as she emerged from the trees, the vehicle now in sight.

She switched back to IR mode and chanced a look behind her.

"No fucking way."

A solid mass of heat signatures moved together now. If Shay hazarded a guess, she would estimate over a hundred pursued her now. The enemy horde advanced steadily but without a quick pace. It's like they had all the time in the world.

She turned back to her truck, the faint thermal differential of the vehicle still distinguishable in IR.

Shay threw open the truck and jumped inside, yanking off her AR goggles with one hand while starting the vehicle with another. The engine roared to life, and she threw the vehicle into reverse before spinning around. It'd be a short distance over the grass and back to the main road.

Her foot pressed the accelerator to the floor, and the truck rushed forward. A few seconds later, the truck shook with an impact and a thump. Then another. Then another.

Even if she couldn't see whoever she was running into, she could see the dents they were leaving in the hood.

The hits ceased, and only the shaking of the off-road travel afflicted the Chevy. Shay arrived at the road and yanked hard on the wheel.

A few minutes later, her heart returning to normal, Shay grabbed the AR goggles and chanced a quick look out the window. Nothing unusual. At least nothing unusual that she could see.

"I think I prefer the naga," Shay muttered.

Shay slowly let out a deep breath. She didn't know what she'd just faced, but she also knew it didn't matter. Her job was to take out the artifact. The mystery horde now would get nothing but pottery shards for their trouble.

Fuck you and your chaos demons. I won.

After stepping out of her Fiat into Warehouse Two the next morning, Shay noticed several of the cubicle walls had been removed from the maze and set in a pile. Peyton was reclaiming the warehouse for work, or he was taking the walls to his apartment.

Peyton waved as he stepped out of the office. "You know, now that I've got my own place. I need to think about getting some better wheels than borrowing one of your creepy vans."

Shay shrugged. "You've got money and know how to hide your trail. Buy a car. It's not like I'm gonna give you my Spider."

"I don't like your car that much anyway."

Shay rolled her eyes. "Please tell me that our mystery evil dude paid up finally."

Peyton nodded. "Oh... one second." He pulled out his phone and tapped away. "Oh, yeah, he did it last night to the secondary account. I'll get it transferred over."

"What the hell?"

"What?"

"You didn't think to tell me?"

Peyton averted his gaze. "I was distracted."

"Distracted by what? Porn? I was getting chased by weird invisible mobs, and you're too busy to pay attention to my stuff?"

"No." Peyton rubbed the back of his neck. "Something important came up."

Shay shrugged. "Like fucking what?"

"My brother, sister, and mother are out of the country." Peyton blurted it out.

"What?"

"You heard me." Peyton sighed. "Look, I've been keeping track of them on occasion. That's a good thing, right? It means I know if they're looking for me still."

Shay shook her head in frustration. "It also means you could potentially mess up, and they could realize that you're still alive. I thought you were smarter than this by now, Peyton."

"I never got to say goodbye to my father. I should at least visit his grave."

"Back to the East Coast? I can't believe you. It's not like you had some great relationship with him. You told me yourself. If it was your mother, that's one thing, but your dad?"

Peyton threw up his hands. "And now he's dead, okay? I think maybe I should try and bury the hatchet in some little way, at least for my own sake."

"How you gonna bury the hatchet with a dead man? You gonna bring along a necromancer?"

"I want to visit his grave. It's a perfect time. My family's out of the country. There's zero risk."

Shay shook her head. "You want to go visit that grave? You're gonna end up in a grave, you fucking idiot. Just because I think it's safe for you to have an apartment doesn't mean I think you should go back to the lion's den. I won't let you."

"Maybe I'm not asking if you'll let me."

Shay marched right up to Peyton and grabbed him by the shirt. "You think you intimidate me, Peyton? I had a fucking invisible mob chase me the other night. A giant cobra tried to eat me recently, and I went to war with an entire gang. Don't try tough guy with me. You can't fucking pull it off." She let go of his shirt and pushed him away.

Peyton stumbled back and looked down at the ground, his face red.

Shay sighed. She wasn't trying to be a bitch, but the risk was too great for a minimum payoff. It wasn't like he'd even get anything out of it. Closure? His brother, at the minimum, still wanted him dead.

"I want to make a deal with you." Peyton forced himself to look up.

"A deal?"

"You go with me to NYC so I can visit my father's grave."

Shay narrowed her eyes. "Why would I do that?"

"Because I know where you can get some adamantine."

"You son of a bitch. You found some, and you've been holding out of me."

Rage mixed with respect. The more Peyton learned

how to set up leverage to protect himself, the longer he'd last if anything ever happened to Shay.

Peyton lifted his chin higher. "If you want to pull a gun and threaten me, do it."

"I just want to understand, if we go to New York, you might die."

"No, I won't."

"How can you be so sure?"

Peyton managed a smile. "Because you'll have my back."

Shay ran her hands through her hair. "You're a fucking idiot, but whatever, you have a deal."

———

Shay continued her IR sweep of the graveyard. Her recent experience in Ohio only reinforced that relying only on one's normal sight to detect enemies might end with one's death. She set up a small tripod connected to an antenna and set it on the ground before flipping the on switch.

She flipped her goggles up and then pulled out her phone to check the LIDAR feed from the black drone hovering about 500 feet above them. As far as she could tell, they were the only people in or near the graveyard. Not that she expected a huge crowd at midnight.

Yeah, going to a graveyard at midnight. With my luck lately, fucking Dracula will show up.

She waved to Peyton in a nearby gray Kia. It was the most non-descript car she could find on short notice.

Peyton stepped out of the car, a pensive expression on his face and a small framed picture of him and his father in one hand and a shovel in the other.

"This is still idiotic," Shay muttered.

"My life to risk."

"Let's just make it quick."

She fell in behind Peyton as he made his way to his father's grave.

HERE LIES WILLIAM ALEXANDER COOLIDGE. LOVING FATHER AND HUSBAND.

Peyton handed Shay the shovel and then stared down at the grave in silence for several minutes as she started digging.

"I know he was a son of a bitch in a lot of ways, Shay. I'm not an idiot. It's just... family is difficult. Thanks for helping with this, though. I think... it's what I needed."

Shay shoveled another pile of dirt from the grave. She didn't care about going six feet down, just far enough that they could hide Peyton's picture. A coming rainstorm forecast for the next morning would hide the evidence they were ever there.

"Family's a weird thing to me." Shay sighed. "My parents were worthless, and I gave up on them when I was much younger than you." She laughed. "Who the hell knows, though? You know it's like Brownstone. That dude has been a lone wolf his entire life, and now he's suddenly inherited a daughter."

"You're sure spending a lot of time with that guy lately. Shit, you helped him rip the heart out of the local Harriken. You into him?"

Shay scoffed and pointed to her hole. "Of course not. Toss your picture in there. You can fill the hole."

Some truths Shay wasn't ready to share with anyone, even the man she now considered a friend.

Peyton dropped the picture into the hole and took the offered shovel. "Not saying there's anything wrong with that. I mean if he looks like what I've seen in the pictures, got a lot of nice muscles. Chicks dig muscles."

"Trust me. It's not like that. Brownstone... it's all professional."

"Helping him kill a bunch of Harriken was all professional?"

Shay shrugged. "Now he owes me, and I can use all those muscles and guns to help me when I need it."

Peyton shoveled some dirt back into the hole. "Whatever you say."

An hour later, Shay parked in an underground lot, miles away from the graveyard. Neither she or Peyton had said much of anything since leaving the graveyard.

"Okay, Peyton. I helped you. Now you can help me."

Peyton sighed. "You know, I would have told you anyway."

"Huh?"

"About the adamantine." Peyton shrugged. "Even if you didn't help me with the grave thing. Not everything has to be a bargain, you know. I just... whatever."

Shay stared at him for a moment and nodded. "Okay, from what you told me on the plane, the guy who has the metal is some sort of collector? This Larry Patino?"

"Yeah. Strange, strange guy. From what I can tell, he collects rare materials and resells them, but he's also ruthless as hell. My research says he got the metal by killing a dwarf who'd been hired to make an item for a different client."

Shay rubbed her hands together. "Then he shouldn't mind if I borrow it from him, but a guy like that has got to have some serious security."

"Yeah. Trying to steal it from his mansion would be suicide, even for you."

"Then we just need to get him on the move with it."

Peyton nodded. "Sounds good, but how?"

"By offering to buy it."

"Yeah, about that... he wants 100 million dollars for it. You're a bit short."

Shay grinned. "Sure, I am, but he doesn't know that." She pointed to Peyton. "You can help me fake being richer for long enough to get this to work."

Peyton's face mirrored hers. "Yeah, I think I can."

"Then we have a plan."

Shay stared into her compact in her hand. Between the colored contacts, make-up, and red wig, she looked like a totally different person, which was probably a good thing considering she was now back in New York.

Complained so much to Peyton about not drawing the eye of the wolf, but I'm about to attract a lot of attention to myself.

She took in a deep breath and sipped her coffee. The café's front bay windows provided a nice view of the shop where Patino was supposed to deliver the metal. On the outside, it looked like any other jeweler in New York, but the place served as neutral ground for the local criminals.

Shay's plan would net her the metal, while stirring up the entire NYC underworld and risking exposure. A fun time all around.

"I've got a visual on the delivery car, nice Lexus." Peyton's voice sounded in her ear through a clear earpiece. Up close it was visible, but it resembled a hearing aid more than anything else and didn't draw undue attention.

Multiple drones patrolled the sky, all under the man's control. Shay might be unused to having someone working direct backup for her, but she couldn't doubt the utility of not having to monitor surveillance feeds herself.

She tossed a few bills on the table and headed toward the exit. The key to the operation would be hitting the target hard and fast. If they lingered, NYPD might show up, SWAT or even an Anti-Enhanced Threat team, and then she'd be screwed.

Shay emerged from the café and spoke into the throat mic concealed underneath her high-necked shirt. "Any change?"

"Nope. Still on his way, he's still got a couple of blocks."

Shay reached into her handbag to confirm its contents, including a gun and a few other surprises. She patted underneath her jacket for her knives.

"Son of a bitch."

"What's wrong?" A hint of panic entered Peyton's voice.

"The damn temporary knives disappeared. Fucking gnome."

"Well, that's all the more reason for you to complete this job."

Shay snorted. "True enough."

Shay made her way down the street. If she wasn't in

position for the attack, the whole thing would be a waste. She wondered if they should have spent more than a day coming up with a plan.

"About sixty seconds out," Peyton said.

"Thirty seconds from the corner." Shay blended in with the flow of foot traffic as she made her way to the intersection. "In position."

"Target is 25 seconds out. Moving drone."

Shay looked up. The stream of drones in the skies of New York City wouldn't be of special note to anyone, nor would it look odd that a single drone broke off and dropped altitude. Everyone would assume it was nothing more than a delivery drone.

Peyton cleared his throat. "Ten seconds. Nine. Eight. Seven. Six. Five. Four…"

A silver drone zoomed down on an intercept course with a black Lexus.

"Three… two… one."

The drone buzzed and collapsed right on top of the Lexus. The car died and the stream of vehicles behind him slammed on the brakes. A few minor collisions happened up the line followed by a loud blare of horns.

The doors to the car flew open and Patino, a stocky, balding man rushed out, a suitcase handcuffed to his wrist. Three large men in suits emerged from the car, guns drawn.

Shay whipped her pistol out of her float print handbag and put a round into each of the guards.

People screamed and rushed away from the battle. There was no way the police wouldn't be there soon.

Shay rushed right toward the wide-eyed Patino and

pointed her gun at his head. "Give me the briefcase in five seconds, or you're dead."

"You have no idea who you're fucking with."

"Three… two…"

"All right. All right." Patino sucked in air through his teeth. He placed his thumb on a small plate on the case and winced, a DNA sampler.

Peyton hissed. "There's a bunch of other vehicles coming up fast. I didn't see where they came from."

Shay didn't respond for a moment, instead keeping her attention on Patino.

The handcuffs around his wrist clicked open, and Shay snatched the briefcase away and sprinted toward her next target at a subway station. Several people screamed and leapt out of the way as three more Lexuses adopted a straightforward strategy for avoiding the traffic blockage and drove up the sidewalk.

"Fuck."

Shay bound down the stairs leading to the subway station. The heavy footsteps of ten men followed her. She turned the corner as three suited goons opened up with their pistols.

The New Yorkers in the subway station screamed and scattered. Shay leapt over a turnstile and spun around to put a bullet into the first two men to hit the bottom of the stairs. The loud report of the shot echoed in the station.

Shay rolled behind a pillar as several other men hit the bottom of the stairs and opened fire. The bullets pelted the metal pillars, bouncing off with sparks. She returned fire and nailed another man.

The plan hadn't anticipated so many reinforcements, but she wasn't worried. She grinned.

Kind of like fighting the Harriken. Taking something from an asshole who shouldn't have it and taking down some underworld scum. Not exactly weeping here.

Shay chanced a quick look at the clock. One more minute. She sprinted for another pillar and laid down more downstream lead at her scattered pursuers. Two more dropped.

Thirty seconds.

The remaining five men advanced and took cover behind their own pillars. Shay reloaded and downed a brave soul a couple seconds later who must have mistakenly thought she was out of ammunition.

They exchanged shots back and forth, the metal and stone pillars protecting the now more cautious men and the always cautious tomb raider.

The roar of the oncoming express train brought a grin to Shay's face. She dropped her gun for a moment and grabbed her last few surprises in her handbag and tossed them toward the men.

A loud bang echoed as her flashbang went off. Several people screamed or groaned. She followed up with two smoke grenades a moment later and ran not for the train, but for a door farther into the station.

Shay ripped off her wig and tossed it into a nearby garbage can. She arrived at a utility access door. An electronic lock denied her entry, but she swiped a small, thin black card, a universal decoder, and it clicked open. The MTA didn't exactly have military-grade locks.

Shay slipped into the door, ignoring the shouts,

screams, and thick smoke wafting around the subway station.

She ran down a narrow hallway and hit a stairwell before pulling out her phone. Once she hit underground, she'd lost communication with Peyton. Ironically, she could just call him thanks to the subway cell stations, but then her phone activity would be geolocated for the police. She needed to leave as few traces as she could.

There was no need to worry. She and Peyton had planned for this eventuality.

"Let's just hope your map is accurate."

A half-hour later, Shay emerged onto the streets of New York, a briefcase in hand, but missing her wig, contacts, and jacket. There was nothing to link her to the earlier attack. By now, the police and local underworld were probably setting up an ambush for the express train and would be very disappointed, if they weren't already.

"Can you hear me, Peyton?"

"Yeah. I'm sorry. Real sorry."

"Huh? About what? I got the briefcase, and no one followed me. This is a win."

He sighed. "Yeah, but ten guys we hadn't planned on showed up. That was close, way too close. They could have killed you."

Shay chuckled. "That wasn't even the closest call I've had in the last few weeks, and at least none of those guys threatened to eat me."

A few days later, Shay grinned at Tubal-Cain as she set the open case containing the gray bars of adamantine on the table in his back room.

The gnome looked her up and down for a moment, his scowl giving way to something approaching a smile. "Impressive and unexpected."

"A deal's a deal, right? You can make the knives?" Shay shrugged. "The other ones you loaned me disappeared."

"Like I said, I wanted to motivate you." The gnome ran a finger along one of the gray bars, an almost hungry gleam in his eyes. "Yes, I can make your knives. They will be well-balanced, almost impossible to break through normal means. They will stay sharp without needing your help and they will be light-weight. But, as I said before, they will cut only what you expect them to cut."

"Fine by me. I'm looking for some reliable knives, nothing more, nothing less."

The gnome harrumphed. "You're short-sighted, like many of your kind, but I still grant you my respect for accomplishing something I thought would be more difficult, Miss Carson."

Tubal-Cain's use of an actual respectful address instead of some vague insult wasn't lost on Shay.

She grinned. "That's kind of my thing. I've had a good run as of late, let's just say."

"I'll keep that in mind. In the future, I might even consider retaining your services for my own needs. For now, though, I'm content to make your knives and offer you your bonus."

Shay nodded. She'd almost forgotten about the offer.

"Mass death has a way of screaming to anyone who knows how to listen," Tubal-Cain said.

Shay's face tightened. "Lots of people die in L.A. everyday."

"Yes, but ancient and powerful magic isn't associated with it."

Shit. Does he know about Nicole? Was it some sort of major magic flare to all the big players?

"I... don't know what you're talking about."

The gnome snorted. "Go ahead and feign ignorance. It's close enough to your natural state, anyway. I think you and your friend have no idea of the power of Oriceran magic."

Shay licked her dry lips. "I've seen the aftermath. Trust me, I don't doubt the power of Oriceran magic."

Tubal-Cain stared at her, his head tilted. "Let me provide you with some helpful information. The Grayson PMC Services company knows they sent many men to kill a single man, and they all died in a horrible way that screams of magic."

She said nothing. The gnome had better things to do than sell her out to other humans. She assumed he was going somewhere with this.

"This is your bonus, Miss Carson. Information. Grayson doesn't know it was a Drow, you see. They have a more practical target, something they understand, a human who might be using magical artifacts."

Shay swallowed at the mention of Nicole's race.

The gnome shrugged. "They think it was the bounty hunter. They've started looking around for ways to increase their power against magic and are talking to some dangerous sorts of people. Very dangerous. I can't say when they'll come for James Brownstone, but when they do, they'll bring powerful magic with them."

She stood. "Thanks for the tidbit."

Now I'm wrapped up with the Harriken and Grayson because Brownstone is. I should be more pissed, but I'm not.

Tubal-Cain eyed her for a moment in silence. "Any more questions?"

"When should I come for the knives?"

"I'll contact you. I have my ways."

"I guess I should get going. I'm sure you have things to do."

"Of course," the gnome replied. "See you around, Miss Carson."

———

"Peyton?" Shay called as she stepped into Warehouse Two. There was no response.

Her phone chimed, and she checked her messages.

Hey, if my facial recognition system is working right, this text should arrive just as you step out of your car. I went out for a bit.

Shay rolled her eyes. He could send her a text without the complicated set-up.

Her phone chimed again.

Oh, and if you're wondering why I didn't just send you a text, I wanted to test the new system. It has applications other than sending messages.

Shay snickered. Boys and their toys.

She wandered into the office to take a seat in front of

the computer. No job or tracing alerts defaced the screen. Everything was calm for once.

After risking Peyton and her own exposure in New York, Shay welcomed a little tranquility. Between the Harriken and her recent tomb raids, it seemed like she didn't have time to catch her breath.

A soft smile came to her face. Money was flowing in, and her tomb raider reputation was only growing. She'd established more contacts, including a gnome, and she'd managed to tweak the nose of the New York underworld without them having any clue it was her.

Her life plan was starting to crystalize into an actual achievable goal. She could earn the money she needed to retire in safety, and much faster than she ever thought possible.

Shay hadn't planned on a few road bumps, including Peyton, Brownstone, and Alison, but she'd dealt with the situations and not ended up dead or exposed, which was all that mattered. She smiled at the thought of all her new friends.

Shay stood so quickly she knocked the chair back. Friends?

She turned the word over in her mind a few times. Yes, *friends*. It wasn't like Bella and her crew, who were just a nice group of girls she could pretend with for a few hours. Peyton and Brownstone knew the brutal truth of Shay's past and didn't flinch away. Alison could peer into her very soul and declared it beautiful.

These people weren't work contacts to be ignored except when on the job. She'd even helped Brownstone avenge his dog and Alison her mother.

There was one unescaped truth confronting Shay.

"Fuck. I don't just have a life plan. I think I actually have a life." She burst out laughing as a smile spread across her face.

FINIS

It's 8:29 p.m. on Sunday night and Zen Master Steve is waiting for these notes. I'm bleary-eyed tired from all the reading, writing, editing, typing I've been doing lately but I'm in the home stretch. Throwing in getting the house ready for sale (and a surprise open house this weekend that I found out about on Monday...). It's true what they say – buying and selling a house is one of the most stressful things you can do. Pile on top of that collaborating in the LMBPN world where time burbs regularly happen and we step through the tardis and BLAM! another book is coming out.

It's all felt like an at home science experiment on endurance – still worth it! I haven't been on the Facebook groups that much this past week but I'm still here, typing away and the snippets totally got away from me. (Does this count as one giant snippet?)

The good news is there are now four, count 'em FOUR series that are all connected to each other in Oriceran. The Unbelievable Mr. Brownstone, I Fear No Evil (that's Shay),

Rewriting Justice (Leira 2.0) and The School of Necessary Magic (hello Alison). I get to see a behind-the-scenes sneak peek at how they're all connected, what's coming next and who's doing what to who and it's some good stuff. Stuff I cannot tell you and will blow your mind when we all get there stuff. That's what keeps me up late at night still typing.

Besides, you guys are funny and touching and share your lives with me online and we've all grown to be a very large, raucous family who share pictures and events – and favorite lines from books. It's the best.

In other news... the new house is coming right along. Drywall is up... brick has not arrived. A few couples came through for the open house and then in dry central Texas the heavens opened up and buckets of rain fell. Still all good. One way or the other we'll all get to the finish line together. Have I said I'm looking forward to when it's the Fall?

Until then, thank you for reading this story. BLAM! Another Brownstone is coming out this week, and then a Leira 2.0 – first one! is coming out next week – and then the first School of Necessary Magic – Dark is Her Nature is out. Then we start it all over again.

In all the 30 years I've been writing I wished, prayed, begged for a time like this and it's more than I could have ever hoped for – I say it all the time but it just keeps getting better and so, I'll say it again. Grateful for all of the Great Fans and for Michael Anderle and LMBPN and his magic Tardis. BLAM! More adventures to follow.

OOOOOO HHOOOOLLLY CRRRRAAPPPPP...

Before I wax philosophically on the right or wrong way to publish and push the envelope, let me say THANK YOU for not only reading this story, but you read all the way through to these authors notes, as well. We try to bring you characters shaped into stories that you will enjoy.

Now, a bit about what is going on...

EXPLOSIONS (of books.)

Here we are, with Shay #2 having already released TUMB 03 (TUMB 04—*Bring The Pain* due out Friday May 25th) and pushing on Shay #3 and Alison's first book, *Dark is her Nature—School of Necessary Magic Book 01.*

We are trying to put out three different connected series (Mr. Brownstone, Shay, and Alison) close together. Mind you, we are trying to do this simultaneously, and further, we hope you find them interesting.

In all, we will do up to thirty-two books. Possibly fewer

Alison (four) / More Mr. Brownstone (twelve) and Shay (twelve) if the Alison doesn't draw as large a crowd (Allison's books are YA.)

Once we get to the end of our efforts on Brownstone's arc, I'll have to take a breather and see if we have told these characters' total stories or not. If we have, great! If we *haven't* – does the customer base 'WANT' a new Brownstone, Shay and Alison and what would it look like?

I am in 'love' with this small family and how they are growing together. I see Shay being able to continue having adventures for as long as enough fans wish to continue reading about her. Mind you, she HAS to change to keep that interesting.

We shall see if Martha, Judith (Berens) and I are up to the task ;-)

Ad Aeternitatem,

Michael Anderle

The Kacy Chronicles

* A.L. Knorr and Martha Carr *

Descendant (1) - Ascendant (2) - Combatant (3) - Transcendent (4)

The Midwest Magic Chronicles

* Flint Maxwell and Martha Carr*

The Midwest Witch (1) - The Midwest Wanderer (2) - The Midwest Whisperer (3) - The Midwest War (4)

The Fairhaven Chronicles

* with S.M. Boyce *

Glow (1) - Shimmer (2) - Ember (3) - Nightfall (4)